the transmogrification of isobel:

a satire

by

grant kuchan

one : pewter hippies

The bedroom had been tastefully appointed. Great pains had been taken to insure that it was opulent without pretension. She said the walls held a delicate balance of negative space that enhanced the modern ascetic. He didn't like the distraction of art. He said that her desire for wall hangings was covetous. She questioned whether he would rather be the one to create a home. He didn't like it when she spoke to him like that. He hated feeling emasculated. He walked away from the conversation after insisting a piece of wood be nailed to the wall over the velvet kneeler in the corner of the room.

The lump of his body caused the designer duvet to rise and fall with his breathing. He hadn't cared for the designs at the stores. The one she had liked, he said was downright lustful. She wondered how a blanket could be lustful? She hadn't meant to say it out loud. He glared at her. His anger bore into her.

An off white duvet, that didn't clash with the eggshell walls, had to be special ordered. It was a nightmare to keep clean.

She hated it. She hated all of it.

The duvet, the room, the choking and sputtering while he slept.

She had recorded herself sleeping. When she slept she would inhale and then exhale. It was peaceful.

His would begin with an inhale, then catch, causing him to gag and sputter before exhaling in a deep sigh.

She stood next to the bed while he slept.

She wondered that if she thought hard enough maybe he would just stop. Maybe if she were to time her wish perfectly, in that moment when his breath caught, he would be thoughtful enough to just stop breathing.

He rejected any indication that he needed to see a sleep specialist. When she recorded it and played it for him, he claimed that it wasn't snoring.

"Yes," she said, "I know technically you aren't, but-"

"But, what?" he said. "This is going to be a fun change, you telling me what to do. You can't tell what's what when you're taking medication. It is even worse when you're not."

"No," she said, "that's not the point."

"Then what is the point? Please, explain to me what is the point?"

"This is all getting away from me again," she said.

"Every single time it is the same thing," he said. "Every time, it all gets away from you. The answer is here in front of you. Right there on the wall!"

She looked at the piece of wood he had nailed to the wall. She wondered if she could snap the pewter hippy off of it and somehow use that. She wondered if she had more of the pewter hippies if she could make a difference. She could have them all rain down on him. It would have to be an awful lot of pewter hippies. Thousands and thousands of pewter hippies raining down and slowly crushing him. Or, one that might be sharp enough, and falling fast enough to slice his jugular.

She thought about using her phone to find the easiest way for little pewter hippies to reach terminal velocity. But, first she would need to find out if terminal velocity is what she actually meant.

Either way there would be a mess.

She had searched four different stores to find the exact thread count in Egyptian cotton that he wouldn't find offensive.

What was offensive about thread count?

That was something else he never bothered to explain to her. What was offensive about a number?

She thought about walking down the hall to check on their son. That used to make her feel better until he said, "It is fucking creepy when you do that."

"What is?"

"When you open the door and watch me sleep," said the boy with the messy blond hair and the bright eyes. "It's fucking creepy. I feel like you're going to murder me."

"It helps me feel safe when I know you're safe," she said. "And please stop saying, fuck."

"Really?" he said. "You, of all people are going to start obsessing over a fucking word?"

"I'm not obsessing," she said. "I just wished you wouldn't use that word."

"Well, I fucking love it," he said.

"Please," she said.

"Please," he mocked. "You know what I'm going to do?"

"What are you going to do? Lock you bedroom door?"

"Nope," he said, his bright eyes wide and full of malice. "I'm going to fucking jack off."

"What?" she said, as her face turned red.

"You heard me," he said. "I'm going to be tickling my dick constantly. If you want to look in on that, fine. But, you've been warned. Now every time you want to feel safe you're actually watching your own son jack off. Pervert. That's right, you want to watch your own son touch himself then there is something fucking wrong with you, but we already knew that."

"I'm your mother," she said. "Please don't talk to me like that."

"Fuck you!"

She hoped it had been an empty threat, regardless at this hour she knew he wouldn't be masturbating. She approached the door, and eased it open. A wave of panic washed over her until she remembered he was sleeping over at a friend's house.

She could see him, the boy from soccer, the one with the happy mom. She tried to remember their name. She remembered their house, the new one on the East side of the development. As it had grown, dominating the little cul-de-sac, her husband told her to, "…not be covetous."

She wasn't.

She was confused. Not over the house, who cared about a house? She couldn't make sense of the happy mom's smile.

She knew it was a lie.

Why? Why do you feel the need to lie? The only people over the age of ten that smile that much are insane, or mentally deficient!

She thought checking her phone to see if that was the right thing to say. She didn't want to offend. She needed to speak respectfully and correctly.

The wave of panic returned. She hated it when her son slept over at someone else's house. He came home extra surly, wondering why she didn't wander the house with a lie plastered across her face, so she could be pretty.

She could walk a little further down the hall and finally open that door.

That door.

The one that had been shut since...

The one her old therapist said she should open.

She wondered if it would even open, or if the dust and the cobwebs had sealed it permanently? Maybe it would become like one of those ancient tombs in the old movies? One day archeologists would dig up her home, and they would pry back the door, and a curse would befall them!

"There's nothing to be afraid of," her therapist said. "It is just a room. Curses are not real."

He was too close. She hated it when her therapist got this close.

"Please," she said, moving away from him, and nearly falling off the couch in his office.

"This is a safe space," he said. She could smell stale coffee and sour rot on his breath.

She would later talk to her husband about finding a new therapist, one that was a woman.

"There is no reason for you to fear an empty room," he said. "All you need to do is walk through the door. You don't have to do anything once you're there. This is just a step in your process to heal. Opening that door, is just the beginning."

She was standing in front of the door. Her hand shook and dripped with sweat as she reached out her hand to grab the handle. Maybe her hand would be so wet it would just slip off?

She could be proud that she had tried.

Even if no one else would be.

She knew no one else would be.

Silently, she ran back through the hall and into the room with the choking mass. Passing it she opened the door to the closet and closed it softly behind her.

She turned the soft light on in the walk in closet and looked at herself in the full length mirror.

Her floor length night gown was warm. She hated how it tangled around her legs, trapping her as she slept. She pulled it off and looked at her body. She was all knees, elbows, and ribs. Bruises surrounded a mole that she had been meaning to speak to her dermatologist about.

Are there dermatologists in the frontier? Should I get it examined before I leave? If I leave? When I leave?

She hoped in the frontier there would be nothing as boring as a dermatologist. Or, as annoying as a therapist. Or, as pokey as a primary care physician. She was done with their pills that made her foggy, and confused. She wanted to talk with witch doctors, and ancient healers that would help her become more, with salves, potions, and magic older than the concrete that her dermatologist's office was in.

That wouldn't be very difficult they only built that strip mall last year. But, magic is magic. Right?

It was a nice strip mall. Not too modern to feel sterile, but not so homey that it didn't feel well sanitized. The huts and teepee's of the frontier may not be sanitized for her protection, but did magical places have to be?

Did bleach kill all of the magic in the world? Should I stop washing my hands with anti-bacterial soap before I go? I could just go back to bed.

He liked how skinny she was. If she woke him, surprised by her naked angles, he would try to fuck her with his inoffensive penis; too quick to be boring and was too small to be threatening.

He would go back to sleep and continue choking.

She would count the hours until she could call the dermatologist.

She sat crosslegged on the floor. She liked how uncomfortable the hard wood floor felt. She wouldn't be able to fall asleep as she sat there.

Eventually, she would have to do something.

She would have to make a choice.

She looked into the mirror, falling into the green eyes that stared back at her, and thought about the lentils.

two : organic french green lentils

To fault the organic French green lentils would be misguided.

Not that placing the fault at the figurative feet of another lentil or legume in the bulk food isle of the upscale grocery store would be appropriate. But, and Isobel would want you to understand, the organic French green lentils are not to blame. Isobel often enjoyed serving them with either some lightly sautéed vegetables, or as a side with a chicken breast, even if no one else did.

No one ever did.

"Why are we eating this again?" said the boy at the table, as he picked at the lentils. "You know I fucking hate them."

"Please don't use that word," said Isobel. "Especially, not at the dinner table."

"You're the dumb ass who served the lentils," said the boy. "If you didn't want me to say the word lentil I won't if you don't fucking serve them."

Isobel would try her best to hide her tears of frustration. She didn't want him to see how much it hurt. It always hurt more when she hadn't been taking her pills. But, when she didn't, it was easier to understand things. She stood up, and walked into the living room.

She let the tears roll down her face in private. If they saw they would know, and make her start taking them again. Why would they want to make her confused?

"What's going on?" said her husband.

"Mom made lentils again."

"Damnit!"

He had left the television on. Isobel turned the volume up, so she didn't have to listen to them. As she glanced at the television, she saw her picture flash across the screen.

The clear voice of an experienced investigative reporter said while her picture continued to dominate the screen, "Experts claim, in hindsight, there was nothing that could have been done; the impetus for violence was within Isobel all along. However, none could agree how her propensity toward such self-destructive behavior initially manifested."

They cut from her picture to one of her as a child standing with her mother. The sight made Isobel cringe as the reporter continued, "Some sighted her upbringing. Her distant and self absorbed mother became an even greater obstacle to Isobel's happiness after her mother had been diagnosed with cancer. It fed her mother's acute persecution complex and a preexisting Messianic complex, making every interaction Isobel attempted with her mother unbearable."

How do you comfort someone who is convinced that her death will cause centuries of unbearable suffering?

Isobel had tried and failed.

"Others point to the tragic events that happened on the beach," continued the reporter as they cut back to the studio. At the mention of the beach, Isobel desperately tried to change the channel, but the remote wouldn't work. "The legislation that followed was a disturbing memorial to a moment of regrettable distraction. The consequence being Isobel's near maniacal focus, fearing that if she didn't pay attention her world might march further into the waiting maw of hell. Implying that Isobel's unyielding vigilance lead to her psychotic break."

A picture of her husband flashed on the screen. She tried to make out his features, but the picture was poorly lit and blurry. "One 'expert' blamed her relationship with her husband, and his obsession with Christian Domestic Discipline. An online exposé explored the well documented incidents, thanks to a hacked web cam, of Isobel finding him masturbating to Christian Domestic Discipline training videos demonstrating the spanking, striking, and admonishing of grown women in the name of Jesus. He was spared, due to his brutal murder, the social media storm surrounding the thousands of memes and gifs created from the images of Isobel's husband masturbating with what is now commonly referred to as a "micro-penis". Support groups were founded in his name, as a reaction to the shaming of Isobel's husband's penis. Across the world men met to support other men with micro-penises."

The picture change to a group of men sitting in a semi circle of chairs in what Isobel thought looked like a church basement. "Not that any of them suffered from a micro-penis, they were there because they wanted to help and show compassion for those who may," continued the reporter, sounding slightly defensive. "Most of the meeting consisted of testimonials, not first hand testimonials, but rather second hand testimonials, and tips that their 'friends' had shared with them on living a normal life with a micro-penis. This consisted mainly of tongue strengthening and agility exercises. However, once the late night talk show hosts began to devote segments of their opening monologues to how sad and comical these meetings were, most support groups disbanded."

A picture of a smart looking woman in glasses appeared on the screen. "Dr. Mamie Allingham's, allegedly definitive account of Isobel's final days in Florida claimed the weird concurrence of events could be easily explained if someone took the time to explore the Quantium Mechanics behind them. Allingham's supposition was that the frequency of the vibrations of a loose lug nut on Isobel's SUV matched that of the excitation of the Higgs field causing the existence of supplemental Higgs Boson particles, effecting the mass of both the SUV and her pre-frontal cortex, as well as creating a well of Quantium micro-gravity around a faulty warning light. These various changes created the conditions which led to everything." Isobel made a mental note to check her lug nuts. "The book topped the bestseller and online 'must read' lists, and for that summer was the center of most dinner party discussions, especially for those who felt the need to feel superior to other people at dinner parties, while they drank varietals of white wine no one had heard of." Isobel wondered what kind of wine they were talking about. "In reality, only a handful of people actually read it. No one wanted to admit that only eleven scientists and mathematicians worldwide knew enough about Quantium Mechanics to understand the book." A picture of five people all in tweed jackets with leather arm patches replaced the picture of Dr. Allingham. "Of those eleven, five of them read half of it and finding the assumptions made in the text flawed abandoned finishing it. Four of them googled how to write, "Higgs Boson" in Hindi, and dared each other to get it tattooed on their forearm." The picture of the people in tweed jackets with leather on the elbows faded into a picture of a tattoo parlor. "The remaining two pointed out, while attending a conference in Bangalore, that their colleague's tattoo didn't actually say, "Higgs Boson" but rather stated, "the God particle," which caused a fair amount of giggling since they were all vocal atheists. None of them discussed the book, but all wished they got invited to more dinner parties."

Isobel sat down, engrossed in this show about her.

"A television psychiatrist prepared to explain how Isobel's behavior could be categorized either that of a psychopath or sociopath, and planned to lead everyone through the Venn diagram he had made to illustrate the important differences between both for his interview for the second hour of Good Morning, Today! Unfortunately, the pet adoption segment before him ran long, and the cooking segment with a celebrity had to begin earlier than expected due to prior commitment from the celebrity. So, no one saw the Venn diagram, and the only thing the psychiatrist could do was talk about the warning signs of a psychopath. The male host joked that the first sign should have been the murder. Most people found this tasteless and insensitive, but everyone had so many other reasons to dislike the male host that no one really noticed."

Isobel felt bad for the psychiatrist. They returned to the studio, and Isobel felt the Investigative reporter looked very familiar. Next to him was Isobel's next door neighbor. She also wondered why this segment was as long as it was. She was flattered that they were taking as much time as they were with her, but she had never been someone who relished the limelight.

"The only person interviewed who had even met Isobel before her rampage across Northern Florida was Marjorie Bateman, her next door neighbor. She would often talk about how Isobel had been awkward, but never excessively strange. Except for the time when they had run into her in the parking lot of Al's Gator World in Kissamee."

"I knew there was something off with her," said Marjorie. "Living next door to her, you get a baseline for someone's normal, you know what I mean. She was fine, she fit in great."

"What do you say to those who state that by turning a blind eye to het abusive husband, you were actually complicit in her psychotic break?" the interviewer would ask.

"I don't buy into any of that," said Marjorie. "Why didn't she say something? You live next to someone long enough you get to know what's really going on. Yeah, they had some issues, especially after everything that happened, but nothing that would lead to this."

"Like her killing her husband?"

"Exactly."

"In fact, Isobel held a great deal of empathy toward everyone she met," said the reporter as he turned away from Marjorie and stared directly at Isobel. "Anyone that suggesting that she didn't have or had a weak sense of right and wrong were misguided. Isobel manifested hallucinations with whom she would discuss the impact of every action she took."

Isobel felt that assessment was harsh. She looked for the off button while the reporter continued, "It wasn't the organic French green lentils, Isobel's mother, Quantum Mechanics, poorly translated tattoos, a hacked web cam, her next door neighbor, her husband, or the micro-penis support groups alone that led to her psychotic break.

No, if any one thing could be distinguished as the impetuous of her violent actions, it was the toe."

The screen went blurry, then Isobel saw herself back in the bulk food aisle at the upscale grocery store. She liked how confidently she walked up the aisle.

"What the hell are you doing?" she could hear her husband say from the dining room. She quickly turned off the television, and walked back into the dining room. She tried to focus in on her husbands's face, but it was just as blurry as it was on the television.

Her son whined at the lentils, while her blurry husband's voice turned into static. She was about to panic then she remembered that she was actually in the grocery store.

Isobel knew that $4.99 a pound for organic French green lentils was an exorbitant price to pay, regardless if there was a human toe in it or not.

She walked up to the tall clear plastic bin tried to touch it. Isobel wondered if the toe could feel her through the plastic. It was a baby toe. Not a toe from an actual baby, but the smallest toe from a grown woman. Isobel wondered if it was actually that small or if the curvature of the plastic was somehow distorting it. Regardless, of how large or small it was, she was very impressed with the intricacy of the nail art on it.

What she could decipher without a magnifying glass was a rainbow attached to a Star of David, with either a unicorn or a narwhal riding behind it. Isobel thought for a moment how thoughtless it was for her to assume the gender of the toe's previous owner. She was about to reframe her entire thought process when she was interrupted.

"Excuse me," said a kid in a green apron. "Ma'am, if you stand right there no one will be able to shop the aisle."

Isobel turned and looked at the kid. If he had only given her another minute she could have gone back and reconsidered the toe without using gender specific pronouns.

Maybe, this clerk doesn't want me to. But, why would he care that I had assumed the gender of the person that the errant toe had been attached? For that matter, how could he know?

Isobel looked at the kid suspiciously. He had a name tag that was larger than necessary. She tried to read the name tag, but the longer she stared, the more the letters danced across it. The first letter which was almost a stylized letter G twisted itself int a D and then in an F. How could anyone learn someone's name from a tag that kept changing like that?

Isobel prided herself on being able to casually notice people's name tags and then call the person by their name in a non-condescending way. She practiced this so as not to come across as privileged or out of touch with people of a lower socio-economic strata.

It rarely worked, but by trying she felt she was doing her part.

"Um," said Isobel, unsure of what to share with the clerk that could not be named.

"Ma'am, you need to move. If you don't move no one will be able to shop the isle." As the kid in the apron spoke he said each word slowly, trying to make sure that she understood.

"But, there's a toe."

"A what?" said the kid.

Isobel pulled out her phone and took a picture of the toe.

"Hey," continued the kid, "you aren't allowed to take pictures in here without the manager's prior approval."

"Why?" said Isobel, hoping that it might buy her a little time. Her new therapist had suggested she take a picture, if things were getting confusing. Isobel was to take a picture with her phone and breathe. Her husband had even thought that it was a good idea. But, there were lots of things that he thought were a good idea that hurt.

Count.

Isobel reminded herself.

She also had to count.

"Then look at the picture," said Isobel out loud. "See if the world starts making more sense, after you take a minute." Isobel didn't like her new therapist. She never felt comfortable talking to her. She always felt that she was either boring her, or wasting her time.

"Where do you think it came from?" her therapist said with a long yawn, as the grocery store melted into her therapists beige office. Isobel had been to enough other therapists to know that the room was intentionally boring. Isobel wondered why her therapists confused peaceful with boring. "The toe," she continued. "Where do you think it came from?"

"From someone's foot," said Isobel.

"That's not what I mean," said her therapist. Her eyes were large and inquisitive, but tired. Her tone was sharp, as if it was helping her stay awake. "What do you think the toe represents?"

"I don't know."

"Think about the toe. What aspects of it stick out in your mind."

Without over thinking it Isobel turned her head and looked at the toe.

"The rainbow," said Isobel, as she returned to the grocery store.

"What?" said the kid. "Lady, if you don't stop acting crazy, I'm going to have to get the manager."

"No!" said Isobel. "That is not a word we use. That word is demeaning, diminishing, and hurtful. Did I say anything that was demeaning, diminishing, or hurtful to you?"

"Not yet," said the kid.

"Just take a minute and look at the rainbow," said Isobel. Isobel realized that no matter how she framed it, this young man wasn't going to recognize the artistry involved with painting something that intricate on a severed human toe. Isobel wondered if he might feel differently if he had to produce nail art that was half as intricate.

Isobel began to feel the black emptiness again. It started in her chest and spread. By the time it reached her fingertips everything made sense.

No one cared.

No one was going to bother to see the rainbow because no one was looking for it. All anyone wanted from the high end grocery store were ethically sourced, artisanal products that were well labeled so that they could avoid various allergens, either out of necessity or because that particular ingredient had been chosen this month to be shunned by various bloggers and celebrities.

No one cared.

All anyone wanted at home was something to eat. They didn't even care about the labels, all they wanted is to put the food they wanted into their mouths.

What if I interrupted them shoveling it into their mouths? Not long enough to deprive them, but just long enough to try to get them to understand? Wouldn't that be fantastic? To go home and tell them all about her day, whether they asked or not! Tell them all about how strange it was.

The toe.

I would giggle and they would steal a glance at that empty fucking chair, pretending I don't notice.

That empty fucking chair! Why did they insist on keeping that chair at the table? Then they would complain.

"I'm going to get the manager," said the kid.

Isobel pulled an oversized organic sweet potato out of her cart and threw it at his head.

"Ow!" said the kid, as an oversized organic sweet potato bounced off his back.

Isobel took better aim with the locally sourced cabbage, and screamed, "But! The! Fucking! Toe!"

Something wasn't right with the world, and from this moment on Isobel was going to do something about it.

Other shoppers who also didn't see the toe looked at each other, hoping one of them would take charge of this unraveling situation. Jumping in to subdue the crazy woman who was slowly emptying her cart one item at a time by throwing the contents at the nice young man who worked there. They were all very disappointed with each other. No one in the aisle did anything to stop the crazy woman. They each hoped that their looks of distain would guilt the other people into learning a lesson on civil engagement.

The young man deflected the items thrown at him using a glass door at the mouth of the frozen food isle.

"Hey," called the muffled voice of the kid from behind the glass door, "somebody call the police! Please!"

All of the shoppers with looks of distain for the other shoppers who weren't doing anything to help the nice young man who was now climbing into the freezer case for protection, wondered why no one was using their phones to call the police. They were all so annoyed by everyone else's inactivity that they pulled their phones from their pockets and began to document everyone else's lack of involvement by taking pictures and short videos that they would later post to their FaceSpace pages and watch as their friends posted about how shocked they were that no one did anything. Validating their annoyance, and shock at the decline of civility in society.

As Isobel threw item after item at the kid, she felt the blackness escaping through her hand. She thought that if she threw enough, maybe she could get rid of all of the blackness. She reached for another item to find her cart empty. She looked around at the other people who were ignoring their full carts and had their phones in front of their faces.

If Isobel stayed, she knew the darkness would devour her world, devour everything.

It was time.

Time to start over in the frontier.

Other shoppers watched a change come over Isobel. They assumed this change would be followed by her coming to her senses, apologizing to everyone, and offering to clean the isle.

Isobel didn't.

three : mile 66

The only remarkable aspect of mile 66 of State Road 90 was the collapsing Orange Juice and Souvenir building. The roof had once been painted bright red with large white letters. An attempt to entice tourists to stop and spend money, before they began migrating via the new high speed interstate freeway. State road 90 was part of a network of roads that had been cobbled together to create an early interstate highway system, and with the exclusion of a twenty-four mile stretch in Texas, almost became the first to cross the entirety of the Southern United States. Starting on the Atlantic coast, in Jacksonville Beach, FL, millions of dollars were invested in a myriad attractions, motels, restaurants, and souvenir stands, across the proposed route.

Thousands of these ventures went bankrupt when I-10 was built only a few miles to the North, before 90 could be completed. Abandoned for more lucrative locations hundreds of buildings dotted State Road 90 sharing a similar fate to the Orange Juice and Souvenir building. The areas of the faded roof that hadn't completely lost its struggle against the encroaching kudzu read, "ange orid." For decades the kids at the local high school in nearby Live Oak knew the "Ange Orid," as fun place to go and drink where your parents wouldn't bother you.

"My brother is back from Tallahassee," would say one desperate teen ager. "He said he'd buy me a sixer and we could head to the Ange Orid."

"I don't know," would respond an unimpressed female teen. "My cousin did that once and was bit by a raccoon. He had to get something like fifteen shots in his stomach for the rabies."

"That's not how they deal with rabies anymore," he would respond, desperate to construct a compelling argument. "And isn't your cousin a senior over in Gainesville?"

"What about it?"

"Well, the raccoon would be dead by now."

"Like you have the slightest idea what the average life span of a raccoon is?"

"No, but I do know what has two thumbs and beer!"

"No, you have two thumbs and an older brother who might buy you beer."

This elaborate mating ritual continued in one form or another, until the advent of the internet. Then teens became too busy creating content to be bothered with underage drinking and premarital sex. The Ange Orid became a target for nostalgic old timers, who began taking bets on when the rest of the structure would collapse, and admonished anyone who was surprised that it was still standing.

"They didn't use that pressboard crap back then," said an old timer, while he stalled in front of the chalkboard in the back of last standing taproom along state road 90. "They used real materials, and made something worthwhile. You head over to those new developments back near Jacksonville and you won't find a single piece of real wood in any of it. Just pressboard crap and plastic."

"I know," said the bartender in front of the board. "If you're not ready to pick a date, Jim that's fine, but I've got other customers."

"Wait, give me one more minute."

"You can take all the minutes you want, Jim. I'm going to go fetch some beer for some folks."

"November 2019!"

"Bold move, Jim," said the regular at the corner of the bar. "You think she's only got a year left?"

"That does sound awfully soon, doesn't it?"

"Jim, I'm not going to tell you what to do with your money, unless you owe me for a beer. Take your time, the pool ain't going no where."

Arguments between the municipalities of Live Oak and Lake City over responsibility for the Ange Orid stalled any hope of either tearing down, or rehabbing it. Regardless, no one could quite remember if the building was owned by anyone anymore. Exercising eminent domain over the derelict, in such an independent minded, and well armed area as Central North East Florida would be political suicide.

So, the Ange Orid sat. A small landmark that made mile 66 slightly different from the rest of route's one thousand six hundred and thirty-two miles.

The night air was aggressively oppressive for a Thursday night in November. It was humid and thick with mosquitoes, moths, and palmetto bugs. At half past midnight the plastic round thermometer that still hung on the corner of the Ange Orid still read in the mid eighties.

Below the thermometer sat something.

A mass of crumpled angles and sequins which had been discarded moments ago by a group of men in a well used pick-up truck.

The truck had bounced along a dirt back road before skidding out onto State Road 90. The vehicle lurching as the tires finally gripped the asphalt.

"Right here?" said the first drunk occupant riding in the bed of the pick up.

"Wait for me to slow down," said the drunk driver.

"Oops. Fuck. Drive!"

The mass tumbled across the weeds and broken asphalt. Under the flickering orange streetlight the sequins created muddy rainbows which pinwheeled around its creator. If the mass had been able to watch the scene from a distance, and still have his sense of humor, he would have mentioned how it looked like a khaki Mormon disco. But, being beaten and thrown from a moving pick-up had a tendency to greatly diminish one's capacity to make a solid joke.

Regardless, he had vowed to stop mentioning khaki. He felt that khaki was a lot like Nazis. To them, any press was good press, and wished both would burn in hell.

A pin prick of light grew into a pair of headlights. The rumble of an engine roared closer. The exclusive SUV passed the Ange Orid at a speed that exceeded the speed limit by more than twenty miles per hour in a blur of beige tartan and elegant styling. The anti lock breaks kicked in fifty meters past the crumpled mass. Loose gravel was kicked up by the massive tires as they fought against the vehicle's momentum. As the car was thrown into reverse, a robotic voice stated passionlessly, "Warning, vehicle backing up, backing up, backing up."

The SUV stopped in front of the thermometer. The engine was silenced, and the cicadas regained their confidence and resumed singing. A middle aged woman, dressed in a simple beige blouse, tasteful knee length pencil skirt, and work boots that were too large for her, exited the car with her phone in her hand. She walked over to the crumpled mass and took a picture.

"Really?" said the mass.

His long legs unfolded from under him, revealing a pair of purple paisley platform heels, and a matching halter top. She didn't mean to think racist, but she was surprised at how tall he was for how Middle Eastern he looked. Most of the people whom she knew that were of Arab descent were average hight or below. Granted all of them were related and worked at her favorite kebob restaurant.

She tried to remember the last time she had gone to the restaurant. She had spent most of the time arguing with a man who didn't understand why she insisted on ordering falafel in a kebob restaurant. She looked at the man in her memory, and tried to remember who he was. She caught a glimpse of his face and saw that it was blank. She wanted to ask if he was her husband, but the memory wouldn't let her.

"Why the fuck would I want to waste my time in that towel head restaurant?" said the faceless man.

"That's not a very nice thing to say," she would say. "I don't think they like to be called that."

"Isobel, you do realize they use your money to fund terrorists?" continued the faceless man, ignoring what she said.

That's right, my name is Isobel! That is something I should remember.

Remembering things became more difficult the further she drove from herself.

"Why would they come all the way to Florida to open a restaurant to fund terrorists?" said Isobel.

"It is basic economics," said the faceless man. He spoke slowly. Isobel couldn't remember why it bothered her so much. "American dollars are worth more than any other currency on the planet, and everyone takes American cash!"

"They didn't when we went to Europe last summer," said Isobel. "Remember they told you to exchange them for Euros, but you didn't, and no one would take your money for anything. I had to go and get the Euros."

"I really don't care for your tone," said the faceless man.

Reflexively she knew that she needed to apologize.

Before things got scary, she brought herself back to the side of the highway.

"Fuck!" as the mass spoke, Isobel noticed that his spit mixed with his blood and pink spittle sprayed in front of him. "You stopped to take a fucking picture? I was thrown from the bed of a pick up truck, and you stopped to take a fucking picture!"

"My therapist said it would help," said Isobel. "She said that if I had trouble understanding if something was real or not, I should take a photo of it with the camera on my phone. Then after I count I should look at the picture. If everything still looks the way I think it does then I know it's real."

"Well, check you, Mary Lou!" he said. "I've always wanted to be a real boy. Just like Pinocchio!"

"My name is Isobel," she said, proud that she could remember.

"What the hell does that have to do with anything?" Isobel watched as more pink spittle landed on the asphalt in font of him. The orange street light made it look off, like it was the blood of an alien.

"My name isn't Mary Lou. I'm Isobel."

"I'm very happy for you."

"Has someone beaten you up?"

"What tipped you off? Did those fuckers ruin my make up?"

"No, it was the blood," said Isobel. "But, they did mess up your makeup."

"I assumed that that was pretty much unavoidable."

"Did they beat you up because you're dressed like a woman?"

"No, they beat me up because I'm Arab."

"Oh," said Isobel. "But you're not wearing a thingy on your head."

"What type of thingy, dear?" he said. "There are lots of thingys. I'm going to need you to be a bit more specific."

"You know," said Isobel.

"I assure you I don't know what 'thingy' you are referring to."

"You're just trying to be difficult and put me on the spot," she said.

"I promise you I'm not," he said. "You don't mean a hijab do you?"

"No," she said. "A head scarf!"

"You sure about that?"

"Positive," she said. "If you're Arab, why aren't you wearing a head scarf?"

"Because, I'm a transvestite sweetheart, not a Muslim."

"I bet not wearing a head scarf would help you blend in, too. Assimilation can be really hard. Where are you from?"

"Plantation."

"Where is that?"

"The wrong side of Ft. Lauderdale."

"Oh," said Isobel. "Are there lots of you people there?"

"Arabs or transvestists?"

"Either."

"Arabs, no," he said. "Transvestites? You'd be surprised. For future reference, saying 'you people' sounds very racist."

"I'm sorry."

"For being a racist or sounding like one?"

"Probably both," said Isobel. "I don't mean to sound like a racist, really I don't. I don't even like it when I think like a racist. You know what I mean? Like how some people may never say anything racist, but they're always thinking it? I think those people are pretty awful. Not to say that I don't have issues. I appreciate you pointing them out to me. How can I learn if you don't?"

"You don't often find people that open to being called ignorant," he said.

"Well, I can't know what I don't know. Someone I know used to say that. I have trouble with my..." Isobel trailed off, distracted by the palmetto bug that was climbing along the wall by the thermometer.

"Do you want to remember?" he said.

"I don't know," said Isobel. "I think the reason I'm headed that way," she pointed back the way she had come, "is to get away from what is that way." She deliberately pointed in the direction the car had been heading. She stretched her arm out, as far as she could get it to go, and then tried to stretch it even further, straining her shoulder and hyperextending her elbow. "But, I'm not sure if I can remember why. Which might be the whole point. If I head back that way I might remember, but I know I shouldn't head back that way. Do you know what I should do?"

"I don't know, sweetheart," he said. "You're the one who forgot it."

"I don't know, either. I don't know if it is healthier to be untethered or grounded by our history."

"All right then," he said. "Live in the now!"

"I like that," she said. "I like that a lot."

"Of course you do," he said. "When freed by the constraints of the past, can we only be truly free to become who we really are. Do we look upon the rose and obsess over the seed that it once was, or do we marvel at its beauty and devour its fragrance? I don't remember who said that or where I read it, so I'll just say it was me."

"I'm allergic to roses."

"Well, then we'll make certain that you blossom into something else."

"Thank you," said Isobel. "Do you need me to take you to a hospital?"

"Do you know where one is?"

"No, but I could ask my phone."

"And what do you think it would tell you?"

"That would depend on what I ask it," said Isobel. "So, do you need a ride?"

"Do you typically offer rides to strange transvestites sitting on the side of the road?"

"No. Nor do I give them to Arabs."

"Well, as long as you're going to be an equal opportunity bigot," he said. "So, tell me bigot, where are you headed?"

Isobel looked down the dark road, and pointed.

"That way," she said.

"West?"

"Yes."

"What's that way?"

"It's away from there," she said pointing the opposite direction.

"Is there any other reason?"

"The frontier is that way," said Isobel. "The way to freedom! Wanna come?"

"Check you, Cindy Lou," he said. "You don't strike me as the Little House on the Prairie type. You seem to be a bit more gated community."

"I don't mean to sound testy," said Isobel. "But, my name is Isobel."

"Are you sure?" he said. "Sounds to me like you're ready to let go of things and soar free like an eagle, sweetheart."

"I thought I was supposed to blossom?"

"Fair point," he said. "I would be delighted to accompany you ma'am."

"What do I call you?"

"What do you mean?"

"I want to ask you your name, but not certain how that works when you're dressed like this, nor am I sure what to ask for," she said. "Do I ask whom you perform under? Do I ask you your stage name? Or is this just who you are when you're made up like this?"

"Aren't we just full of surprises?" he said. "My name is Vincent."

"Really?" said Isobel, sounding disappointed.

"Yes," said Vincent.

"Sorry, I just figure that you would have a more ethnic sounding name," said Isobel.

"Like Abdul?" said Vincent. "Something more Arab sounding?"

"Yes."

"I think I'm just going to get into the car now if that's alright," said Vincent.

"Sure," she said, helping him into the passenger seat.

She gently closed his door, then ran around to the driver's side, excited to have some company.

"Holy fuck! It looks like a kilt vomited in here!"

"The tartan pattern was part of the exclusive limited edition version of the car," said Isobel.

"So you actually paid extra for this?" said Vincent.

"Yes, lots," said Isobel, as she started the SUV. Signaled and pulled back onto the deserted road. "Do you prefer gender non specific pronouns?"

"Aren't we just the enlightened little racist?" said Vincent.

Isobel wilted.

"Oh, now," continued Vincent. "I'm not going to apologize, so you can just stop pouting."

"You could be nicer about it," said Isobel.

"When you said that my name wasn't Arab enough, that was just delicate as one of Nana's doilies. Just because you aren't as bad as the white trash that beat the shit out of me and dumped me on the side of the road, doesn't give you a free pass to be casually racist. I'm not here to help you feel better about your European colonial bullshit."

"Sorry," said Isobel.

The sound proofing in the cabin of the SUV made the extended silence more awkward than it normally would have been.

"One thing I can not abide is a racist asshole," said Vincent, breaking the silence. "I have no patience for them. Racist assholes and cargo shorts are an a-front to everything that is right and just in this beautiful country of ours. I prefer male pronouns. I am not going to go into why I do, I just fucking do. And although I appreciate you asking, it doesn't forgive previous transgressions, but it does illustrate that you are willing to evolve. Luckily we are early enough in your blossoming, that there may be hope for you yet."

"Thank you," said Isobel. "I'll try to remember that."

"You aren't planning on killing me and tossing me in the back of the SUV are you?"

"No," she said. "There wouldn't be room."

"Take a good hard loot at that cargo space," said Bob. "You could haul a good number of groceries home in that. Or, plenty of equipment for the soccer game."

Bob stood at the rear of the SUV. The exclusive tartan pattern wasn't what Isobel had asked for. Isobel thought it was strange that she could remember Bob, the car salesman, his salt and pepper hair, his middle aged gut, and how he smelled like tuna, but couldn't remember her husband.

Bob didn't seem to be a fan of the Florida heat.

"You seem to be sweating an awful lot," said Isobel.

"Don't worry about that," said Bob. "My high blood pressure, and my fat ass don't much care for this current heat wave. But, that it why I am on a strict diet, nothing but tuna."

"That explains the smell."

"Oh," said Bob, his face turning brighter red with embarrassment.

Isobel felt guilty and changed the subject, "I'm not saying it isn't a nice car. I just don't want to pay that much for a car that I didn't order."

"You are going to love this car," said Bob. "The number of safety features are going to make you feel so secure when you're carting the kids around."

"I'm not saying that," said Isobel. "What I'm saying is that it isn't the car that we ordered."

"I understand," said Bob. "Maybe you should talk to your husband about it."

"I should," said Isobel. She tried to picture his face, his build, anything. All that she could remember was his anger. His vindictive, piercing anger that that made her shake. Why did it have to go that far? When did she ever agree to-

"Gas," said Vincent.

"What?" said Isobel.

Is this was why they said I shouldn't drive anymore?

"That blinking light on the dash," said Vincent. "It means that we need to stop for gas."

"That's a fantastic idea," said Isobel. "I need to pee."

"Can I ask you a very personal question?"

Isobel thought about the "very personal questions" she had been asked in the past. If she was going to answer his question about his forthcoming question, she needed to give it honest thought. There was the time when her son had asked her why she was such a bitch. Her husband had once asked what the fuck was wrong with her. There was even the time her mother had asked her why she got such joy in hurting her.

A sign that read, "CHEAP 24, GAS, FOOD, 'n MORE!" invaded her sightline and interrupted her. Isobel thought about being cross with the sign. There had been someone else, somewhere else that had stopped her thought process. She couldn't remember what had happened after that, but she could remember the black that came before it. Isobel placed herself deep in her chest to see if there was more black there.

There wasn't any.

Isobel wondered if the black was having trouble reaching her this far from Jacksonville, the same way that her memories were became faint whispers, nothing more than a nagging breath on her ear. Isobel thought maybe the further she got the better things would continue to be. Maybe she was just imagining it.

Do I count as a thing, too?

Isobel looked at the blinking red light on the dash board.

Had it always been shaped like a gas pump? Or did it only start to look like a gas pump when Vincent had told her what it meant? Did I just find my best friend? Is this the way the world changes when you find that one right person to help you with all of this?

"I'm not sure if we should stop there or not," said Vincent. "But, it doesn't look like we have much choice. I sure as shit am not going to push this car in these shoes. And with how tiny you are I don't think you could."

Isobel smiled. Vincent wasn't frightened of her. He didn't understand the black, or maybe he couldn't see it.

"I'm excited to see what the 'n More is."

"Oh, I think we are in for some disappointment."

The station had at one time been painted something other than a dingy grayish green, but a constant assault by the sun during the day and the fluorescent lights in the evening had taken its toll. Inside housed a magazine rack that was living in denial; its unwillingness to admit to the existence of an internet meant it was crammed full of dusty magazines creatively named after aspects of the female form. A cooler in the rear struggled against the late night humidity to give its customers a choice between warm, and slightly less warm beer. The stereotype behind the counter stood before a large selection of tobacco, condoms, and scratch off lottery tickets, wearing a mesh baseball cap and a t-shirt that would be seen as fashionable if worn by a man ten years younger with a thick beard in an urban area, but looked dated and threadbare on him. He quietly flipped through one of the dusty magazines.

He only looked up because he heard Isobel's phone take a picture. He stared at the woman in the dirty clothes and the man with blood down his purple halter top.

"Hello," said Isobel.

"You can't take pictures of the magazines," said clerk.

"I wasn't," said Isobel.

"Well, whatever it was you were taking pictures of, stop it."

Isobel took a step closer to the clerk and red his name tag. She had once read how it helped people who worked retail feel a greater connection to the people they were helping is you used their names.

"Sorry about that, Gee-off," said Isobel. "May we use your bathroom?"

"For customers only," said Geoff. "And my name's not Gee-off, it's Geoff, pronounce it like it was spelled J-E-F-F."

"Sorry didn't mean to offend," said Isobel.

"You know you would be surprised how many brain dead assholes get that wrong," said Geoff. "You'd figure with all those commercials for that toy store, you know the one with the giraffe, that everyone would realize how to pronounce it."

"So, your mom named you after a giraffe?" said Vincent.

"Fuck you, fagot," said Geoff. "No, she didn't name me after a giraffe, it is a family name."

"Thank you for that nugget of local history," said Vincent. "We are going to fill up, but we would both like to use the facilities and freshen up."

"Well," said Geoff, "before I give you the key you need to understand that we have some very strict policies regarding the use of our restrooms here at Cheap 24."

"You're reading a copy of *XXL Ebony Juggs*, but you have a strict bathroom policy?" said Vincent.

"Hey," said Geoff, "do you see that sign over there through those fake eyelashes of yours? It says we reserve the right to refuse service to anyone. And right now you are anyone, understand sweetheart?"

There was an edge to his voice that made Isobel cringe.

"After all of these stringent rules that bathroom had better be spotless," said Vincent.

"Rule number one," said Geoff, "you use the restroom one at a time. I don't want anybody fucking in there, because I have to clean them."

"That won't be a problem," said Isobel.

"Rule number two, you use the bathroom based on the junk you have, not the junk you want to have."

"Fine," said Vincent. "Can we have the key, please?"

"Show me," said Geoff.

"Show you what?" said Vincent.

"Your junk," said Geoff.

"What?" said Isobel.

"Look I don't know you," said Geoff. "For all I know you both might be men, so I need to see what you've got under there, before I let you use the bathroom."

"I don't think we need to go that badly," said Vincent. "We'll just fill up and then we'll be out of your hair."

"No, you won't," said Geoff. "See, that sign means that I get to decide who I sell to and who I don't."

"I don't think that it does," said Isobel.

"I don't remember asking you!" said Geoff. "You want to fill up? You want to buy a stick of fucking gum in this store? Then show me."

Isobel felt the black beginning to grow in her chest. The longer she spoke to him the faster it would spread.

She looked over at Vincent. His hands shook, as he stifled a whimper. It was strange to Isobel that a creature as large and beautiful as Vincent would be frightened of anything.

Isobel pulled down her shorts.

Geoff's eyes stared at her crotch.

"Done?" said Isobel.

"Now him," said Geoff.

Vincent pulled up his skirt. Isobel averted her eyes out of courtesy.

"That wasn't so bad, now was it?" said Geoff.

Isobel handed him a credit card and said, "I'm filling up while my friend uses the bathroom, please."

"Feel free ma'am," said Geoff.

Isobel stepped back into the humid night. A swarm of bugs attacked the light above her. The gravel crunched under her feet as she walked to the SUV. On auto pilot she removed the gas cap and inserted that nozzle and began filling the SUV.

Her watch vibrated, a reminder sent from her phone. She knew what it was for. She ignored it, closing her eyes. The vibration on her wrist was soothing, it reminded her of her childhood, she couldn't quite remember what. She tried to focus on the memory, but every time she tried to interpret it, it faded into the white noise in her head. She liked to think that it was snow on an old television set. She missed that, with the new technology everyone looked, blocky or pixilated when there was interference. She had heard once that the snow was actually background radiation left over from the big bang. So, the origins of the universe were bleeding into whatever situation comedy she had been watching as a kid. The history of everything right there in front of a bunch of puppets and a musical guest.

Vincent yelled.

Isobel looked up to see Geoff pushing Vincent.

The black swept through her.

The tank was full.

After returning the nozzle and securing the gas cap, she opened the back of the SUV. She had to shift the body to reach the tire iron. She marched toward the argument, pressing a button on her key fob. The tailgate began to close.

BEEP! BEEP! BEEP!

Isobel turned back to the SUV and saw an arm in the way of the tailgate. She absentmindedly threw the arm in and slammed the tailgate closed. The hand slapped against the glass then fell. Satisfied that it was secure, she continued.

Isobel opened the door and entered the air conditioning.

"If you keep this up, faggot, I'm calling the fucking cops," said Geoff.

"For what?" said Vincent. "What the hell have I done?"

"You propositioned me," said Geoff. "I've got you on the cameras flashing your junk at me. I know prostitution is illegal, but solicitation regarding sodomy around here is going to land that hot ass of yours in jail for a very long time."

"Fine call the cops," said Vincent.

"I bet you'd love to be locked up with a bunch of other fags," said Geoff.

"No," said Vincent, "but I think I have a better chance explaining what happened to a police officer that continuing to talk myself in circles with braindead hick."

Isobel would later say that she had only meant to knock the cell phone out of his hand. That she didn't want him to call the cops. The black inside her must have reached the hand that was holing the tire iron, because it was a very well aimed blow to his temple. Geoff's eyes rolled into the back of his head and he fell. His head bouncing off the counter next to his copy of *XXL Ebony Juggs*, with a sicking crack. The body slumped to the floor.

" Fuck!" said Vincent.

"Was it just me," said Isobel, "or was he not a very nice person."

Vincent looked for a flicker of malice, or sarcasm in Isobel's face, but all he could find was her uncensored sincerity.

"No, he wasn't a very nice person."

His reassurance caused her face to break into a bright smile. "Would he be considered a racist asshole? He's wearing cargo shorts."

"Yes. However, not every racist asshole wears cargo shorts."

"I'll try to remember that. Thank you."

Isobel moved behind the counter.

"What are you doing back there?"

"Paying for our gas," said Isobel, as she found her husband's credit card. She tried to read the name off it, but as she did the letters danced around and rearranged themselves. "Do you think we should grab some water or something?"

Vincent looked at the cooler and saw nothing but beer.

"I don't think they have any," said Vincent. "Do you think that it will be a good idea to pay. They'll know you've been here. With everything that has happened, especially with him. I don't think you want him, or people like him to find you."

As Isobel began to tear up, she said, "I knew you were going to be a true friend. Thank you! But, don't worry, it's my husband's card. At least I think it is." She ran the card through the ancient credit card reader and waited for approval. "I'm sorry," she continued. "Is there anything else you might want? I'm not a fan of smoking, but if you'd like a pack of cigarettes."

"That might not be a bad idea," said Vincent.

Isobel pulled out a plastic bag and began filling it with various brands of cigarettes, then handed the bag to Vincent. The credit card machine chirped its approval. Vincent picked a brand from the bag. He looked at the familiar looking desert on the package and smiled. It had been a long time since he had smoked, but with the way the day seemed to be heading, now seemed like a fantastic time to start again. Methodically, he tapped the pack of cigarettes against the heel of his hand, tore back the foil, placed a cigarette into his mouth and lit it.

He inhaled deeply.

Pulling it out of his mouth he wasn't sure if it was his lipstick or blood on the beige filter. He felt slightly light headed and giddy as he went in for more.

"I'm ready when you are," said Vincent through a cloud of smoke.

"I still have to pee," said Isobel.

four : bolt cutters

The floor hurt.

She stood up. She liked how she felt in her bare feet. She was more stable. She didn't trust shoes. They put something between here and the earth.

In the corner of the closet was a roller bag. She tried to remember if it had been a wedding present, or if she had purchased it recently. The wheels on the bottom looked new. She gave it a light twist and the bag spun freely on the floor. She smiled as if it were a toy. She gave it another twist and it spun faster. She wondered what the wheels were made of, and marveled at how fast it could go.

What if I just leave?

That would be a choice of sorts. She could open the bag right now and fill it with her favorite clothes.

"You're not taking any of that," he would say. She wouldn't try to wake him, but somehow he would know. Somehow he would wake up and demand things. He was always demanding things.

"I'm just taking these," she said. "It's just some t-shirts, and some changes of underwear."

"None of that is yours," he said. "I paid for every last stitch. You show me a single sock that you paid for and you can have the entire closet!"

"Please," she said.

"Please," he mocked. "Please? You want me to just go back to bed while you walk out? Have you given any thought as to what this would do to our family? Haven't you already done enough?"

"I'm not trying to hurt you." she said. "I'm not trying to hurt anyone. I just need to go. Please."

She was often surprised at how fast he could move when he wanted to. He was next to her so quickly it made her jump. One hand closed around the handle to the bag, the other raised up to strike her.

She looked into the hot anger in his eyes.

His face becoming more flush.

These were the moments where he said he couldn't stop. Later he would pray, hoping that it would make his anger go away. She had never thought it was strange, until right now, that he never tried to pray her bruises away. Why would it occur to her that he needed to ask for anything more than self control, or to make her more patient with him.

She felt her connection to the ground, her naked feet grabbing energy from the dead hardwood under them. If she concentrated she knew she could be faster than he was. She had been practicing.

Not planning. Never planning, only practicing. Planning is premeditation.

She moved sideways, letting go of the bag, and ducking out of the way of his hand.

Without her grip on the bag to stabilize him, the momentum from his anger caused him to lose his balance. Falling backwards onto the dead hardwood floor that feed her with the power to dodge his blows, was unyielding and as his head bounced off it at a painful angle.

As he lay there, she wondered if he had broken his neck?

It would have been very thoughtful of him if his neck was just broken.

I just watched.

This isn't a plan, this is hoping a plan presents itself. There had been too much passivity, too much inaction. Hard choices needed to be made. Plans and plots needed to be debated and implemented, no matter how messy, no matter how premeditated it may appear.

She walked out of the closet and moved silently across the room as he continued to choke, gasp, sleep. Out in the hallway she pulled the bedroom door shut. She took a quick inventory of anything on this floor that might be useful, before heading downstairs. There were plenty of cleaning supplies, but nothing that she could use without more planning, or skill.

On the kitchen she walked toward the knife rack. There held to the wall with strong magnets were the heavy meat cleaver and the good butcher's knife.

"We need to sharpen the knives," she had told her husband last week.

"Okay," he said. "What do you want me to do about it?"

"I was hoping that you might be able to take care of it," she said. "Thanksgiving is right around the corner, it will make everything a lot easier for me."

"Will it make any of it taste better?" said the young boy with the bright eyes.

She waited to see if he was going to come to her defense, if he were going to look up at her and say that was not acceptable for the bright eyed boy to talk to her like that. No one said anything.

She held the cleaver in her hand and knew that it wasn't going to be sharp enough.

Even if it was sharp, will the memory ruin it?

Having never actually killed anyone before she wasn't sure if she should use something that held meaning, or if an item devoid of secondary intention might be better? She decided to keep the cleaver, as an option.

The hallway closet had an aluminum baseball bat.

"I don't know why you love to torture me like this," said the bright eyed boy.

"How am I torturing you?" she said.

"Do you really have to take me to my game?" said the bright eyed boy.

"Yes, how else are you supposed to get there?" she said.

"Call one of the other moms and tell them you're on the rag or something, and you need them to give me a ride, because you're all out of fucking tampons."

"First, no. Second, please don't talk like that."

"Fuck!" said the bright eyed boy, as he rubbed his temples. "Look, when you're there everyone is on eggshells. Nobody knows how to talk to you, and no one is sure if you're going to freak out."

"I'm not going to do that," she said.

"How do you know? How could you possibly know if you were going to go kind of crazy? It's the surprise of it makes it all that helps put the fun in dysfunctional!"

That would be interesting. Even bordering on fun.

She carried the bat with her, while noting the impracticality of the hockey stick and soccer ball.

She couldn't think of anything connected to the metal poker that sat next to the fake fireplace. It felt sturdy enough in her hands, but she knew she couldn't trust it. It was actively contributing to the shared delusion that the fireplace was real.

She walked out the side door and into the attached garage. She placed each item on the cool cement floor, but before evaluating each of them she gathered a pair of pruning shears that had belonged to her mother and an electric leaf blower that her husband had never even taken out of the box.

With them displayed before her she began to weigh practicalities and ramifications of each potential murder weapon.

But, then she saw the bolt cutters.

The heavy three foot bolt cutters.

Bolt cutters that she had purchased to cut a lock off the gate.

Not a lock that the bright eyed boy had placed there.

Not a lock that he had placed there.

A lock that had just appeared one day. She didn't ask for help. She didn't ask permission. She had gone to the hardware store and purchased them herself, come home and removed the lock.

The bolt cutters were hers, and beautiful.

five : one dozen vegan cupcakes

He slammed the door behind them.

The sound made Isobel jump. She looked around the living room. It looked different then it had when she left this morning.

Is this the right home?

"Why did you do that?" said Isobel, as she turned to face him. His face was gone, in its place was a blank flesh colored oval.

"I was at the cupcake place, and thought-"

"Really?" he said. "It didn't look like you really give it any thought?"

Was he always this tall?

"Wait," said Isobel, as she backed away from him. "I was just-"

"You were just what?" said her husband.

Isobel was confused why she couldn't make out any of his features, as the figure began walking toward her. She could remember how parts of face were supposed to look. The way his eyebrows would furrow, making his forehead wrinkle always made him look older than he really was. The way he turned red when he was angry or embarrassed. Isobel tried to remember if he had kind eyes.

She didn't understand why she couldn't see it. Why she could only see a blank flesh covered oval. Like the way a kindergartner or a minimalist artist might draw a stick figure.

"I was doing the shopping," said Isobel.

"Okay," said the faceless figure. "Do you need help with the groceries?"

"No," said Isobel. "I didn't get any."

"Why?"

"Well, there was this toe," she said.

"A what? A toad?"

"No," said Isobel, as she pointed at her foot. "A toe."

"Thank you. If it weren't for you pointing I might never have realized what human toes are. Tell me were these toes on people's feet?"

"No, they were in with the organic French green lentils," said Isobel. "It had a beautiful design on it. It was so intricate for such a small toe. It had a rainbow-"

"Damnit, Isobel! Did you take your pills before you went out?"

"I never do if I have to drive," said Isobel. "It says right there in the warnings to not operate heavy machinery or drive. After, the grocery store I drove to the cupcake place. But, I don't remember how I got there."

"And then you decided to drive to an elementary school? With a bunch of cupcakes, and you wonder why they would call the cops on a crazy lady who keeps wandering onto the campus?"

"Please don't use that word," said Isobel.

"What word?" he said.

"Crazy," she said. "You know I don't like it when you use it."

"You don't like it that I call a spade a spade?" he said.

"Why don't you care that those words hurt me?" said Isobel.

"Of course I care," he said. "If I didn't care, we could just move on. If I didn't care, I would just feed these things that run around in your head instead of trying to make you better. You're broken Isobel. I'm just trying to put you back together. Why won't you let me help you put yourself back together?"

I'm not broken.

Isobel backed further out of the room.

"Why do you fight us every step of the way," he continued. The timber of his voice becoming sharper. His words cut into her, deeper with each syllable. "I pray on it. I talk to Pastor. I let you talk with a string of therapists! This one is too secular, this one brings us Jesus too much, this one wants to fuck me! Then we find one, and she gives you medicine that you don't even take!"

"Please stop yelling at me."

"No," he said. "If I don't yell at you, nothing changes! Nothing! This is what you need!"

The flesh colored oval began to shift redder.

"Please stop yelling."

"This is the only thing that is going to fix you! Do you understand that? Yelling is the only thing that works!"

"Please stop."

"You knew what I was going to need from you," he said, as he removed his belt. "You know the rules! This is the only way to make sure you remember the rules."

"Please," said Isobel, as she ran upstairs and into the bedroom closet. She pulled the door shut.

"Really?" she heard him bellow as he walked up the stairs. Isobel wondered how he could walk so quietly. "Let me guess you're back in the closet again, aren't you? Like a child. I hate it when you act like a child, there is nothing more infuriating! Just let me fix you."

I'm not broken.

He whipped the door open.

Isobel curled up in a ball and closed her eyes tight. She prepared herself for the first blow, or for him to grab her by her hair and drag her out of the closet.

Isobel looked up.

She used to like the faux Spanish look of the strip mall. It helped everyone pretend that there was historical context to the development, which used to be an uninhabitable swamp. Today, for the first time she noticed how the fake stucco was crumbling, revealing the cinderblocks underneath. Its naïve deception exposing that the building was trying too hard. No one liked an obsequious building.

A sign in front of Isobel read, "Parking for Amy's Cupcake Boutique only!" Isobel thought that the exclamation point was more aggressive than it needed to be.

Am I in the right place?

She tried to remember driving to the strip mall, but couldn't. Isobel hated it when she couldn't remember things. It was happening, more and more lately. Looking at her watch she felt the panic begin to creep. If left unchecked, she knew the panic could become the black.

What am I forgetting?

Isobel got out of her car.

If I move with purpose and intention, maybe everything will become clearer.

Isobel confidently walked into the cupcake boutique. The interior was a blinding collection of white and pink tile. It smelled slightly off. Not bad, but manufactured, like they were using air freshener that was supposed to smell like cupcakes baking, and lots of disinfectant. A young woman in an apron looked surprised at the woman who ran into her store. Isobel tried to remember if she was Amy or not. As she did she could faintly hear someone singing, "Happy Birthday."

That makes sense.

She could see the paper, with all of the guidelines. Precisely how many needed to vegan (twenty-four), how many needed to be gluten free (six), and, of course, all of them had to be nut free. At the bottom of the handout were a list of local bakers that could easily accommodate the requested cupcakes, whose practices had been properly vetted by the local school board to minimize risks to students. Amy's Cupcake Boutique had bee the first one on the list.

"I'm here to pick up a special order," said Isobel. "It's for a birthday."

"I'm sorry but, I don't have any special orders today," said the young woman who might be Amy.

"That's impossible," said Isobel, drawing up to her full height, "I need twenty-four vegan cupcakes, six gluten free, and, of course, they all need to be nut free, for a birthday party at my child's school. And I think I might be late, but I'm not really sure."

"Oh," said Amy, "I only have one dozen vegan cupcakes. "

"Can you make more?"

"Sure, but it will take at least an hour."

"Fuck!" said Isobel, trying to remember when she was supposed to drop them off. "Can you make up the balance with nut free ones?"

"Sure," said the woman. "I can put together thirty cupcakes for you."

"What about gluten free ones?"

"Sure," said the woman. "I have six of those, easily."

"Beautiful," said Isobel.

"But, I can't in good faith sell you these."

"Why?" said Isobel.

"You can't just walk into a school claiming that the cup cakes are vegan when they aren't," she said.

"Does it really matter?" said Isobel.

"Yes, it matters," said Amy. "These children's parents have either made a philosophical choice, or you're dealing with allergies. You can't be so dismissive."

"I understand that you're embarrassed," said Isobel. "I mean this is all your fault. You're the one that lost the special order."

"No," she said. "I don't have a special order for today. These cupcakes are going into a box with my name on them, if it makes someone sick, that's my reputation."

"What if we just put them in a plain box?" said Isobel. "I can tell everyone that I baked them."

"I will not collude with you to deceive children."

"I need those cupcakes," said Isobel.

"I'm not selling them to you," said Amy.

Isobel walked behind the counter.

"What are you doing?" said Amy, as she grabbed the phone and ran to the other side of the store. Isobel looked under the counter and pulled out a pink and white bag with the Amy's Cupcake Boutique on the side of it, and began filling it with cupcakes. "I told you, I'm not selling you those cupcakes," continued Amy.

"Okay," said Isobel, as she continued to fill the bag.

"That's stealing," said Amy.

"Not if I leave my credit card it isn't," said Isobel, as she fished a credit card from her purse and placed it on the counter. "I'll be back for it later. I'm sorry I don't have time for this right now."

"You are deranged," said Amy. "I mean there is seriously something very wrong with you."

I know that. Why would you think I don't know that? But, if I don't do this the black rises up.

"I'm sorry," said Isobel, as she ran to her car with the bag of cupcakes.

Pulling out of the specially marked parking spot, Isobel saw Amy's wobbly hand trying to hold a phone to her ear.

She pulled out into traffic and thought about her options for getting to the school. She didn't want to take the interstate. Driving too fast something might happen to the cupcakes. She flipped on the radio.

"Fuck," she said, as the SUV hit a speed bump in the elementary school parking lot faster than she had meant to.

She hadn't remembered driving to the school. She was afraid that this may become her new normal, constantly driving places and forgetting what happened.

A knock at the car window made her jump.

The man standing on the sidewalk smiled warmly at her. She liked his smile. He waved in a childlike manner. It wasn't dignified or rehearsed, just contagiously enthusiastic.

"Yes?" she said, smiling as she opened the car door.

"Are you here to vote today?" he said.

"I didn't realize there was voting today," she said. "I guess that makes me sound like a stereotypical soccer mom, doesn't it?"

"You are registered to vote, aren't you."

Isobel had to think about that, then she remembered that when she had updated her drivers license.

"What party?" said the woman at the DMV sitting behind a high podium on a bar stool. Her manicured fingers clicked across the keyboard to her computer. The intricate designs on her nails distracted Isobel. "What party?" she repeated. Her monotonous cadence, beguiled her lack of patience.

"I'm here to renew my drivers license," said Isobel, afraid that she had waited in the wrong line. This was the type of thing that her husband would get irritated with her about, wasting time in the wrong line. Like when she would get into the wrong checkout like in the grocery store, or the first class security line at the airport, and no one would let her know that she was in the wrong line until she got to the front of it. How hard would it be to let someone know that you might just be in the wrong line? Why did it always become her fault?

"Everyone is," said the woman, as she rolled her eyes.

"I don't understand the question."

"Which political party would you like to be affiliated with?" she said. "When you renew your license you are automatically registered to vote."

"Is that new?"

"Nope."

"I'm not certain," said Isobel. "Should ask my husband? He's at work. He's a Republican, should I be one too?"

"Not something I am legally allowed to answer for you," said the woman at the DMV. "I'm just here to provide you with options."

"Can I be an Independent?"

"You can be what ever the hell you want, but you have to pick an affiliation. I've got everything from Libertarian to Communist."

The man behind Isobel, sighed heavily.

"No sir," said the woman behind the podium. "You do not get to rush this young lady."

Isobel looked behind her at the man who was vocally annoyed with her. He was middle aged, greying slightly, and expanding more than slightly. She wondered what made his time was more important than hers. He obviously made more money than she did, but not much more than her husband did. Isobel understood that he had more responsibilities that she did, but didn't understand why he felt his time was more important that her's. Unless he had made similar assumptions about her. She wondered what kind of assumptions someone might make about her, and remembered the man that was in the school parking lot waiting for an answer.

"I'm a registered Republican, like my husband," she said.

"Fantastic," he said, as he helped her out of the SUV. "Looks like you got into a bit of a fender bender."

"What?" she said.

"See right here on the bumper," he said. He pointed to a dent in the bumper. There were large scratches all along the passenger side of the car.

"I wonder how that happened?" she said. "I always try my best to be as safe a driver as I can."

"I'm sure you were," he said, as he handed her a piece of paper. "Now, hopefully you've discussed this with your husband, but if you need some help remembering who you are supposed to vote for this flyer has all of the names of the approved candidates."

"Oh," she said, happy to have a way to remember whom she was supposed to vote for. She had a discussion, over lasagna, about the current political climate. She knew there was the man with the bad hair who had the television show, and the woman who nobody liked, because her husband had an affair. She didn't remember much past that, she wasn't certain if it had been her husband she had discussed it with, so the sheet was sure to help. "Thank you." She smiled when she said it. She found most people responded well to her when she smiled.

She followed the signs that read, "Vote Here!" They had large helpful arrows. Isobel liked how each sign's arrow was a different color. One looked like it had been colored in with yellow highlighter pointed to a pair of brown double doors. Isobel remembered how much she had loved highlighters when she was in high school.

The gymnasium was full of voting machines. The wood floor was in the middle of being refinished. The controversy regarding the old Blue Devil mascot had quickly gotten out of hand.

"We are paying good money to a Christian school for them to promote devil worship?" said a shrill woman at the PTA meeting.

The assembled crowd nodded in agreement.

"Did no one put two and two together?" the shrill woman continued. "How hard would it have been to take a moment to be slightly more sensitive to issues like this?"

It took a solid month of polling the parents, students, and surrounding community until they had finally decided on a new mascot.

Isobel was happy with their choice. She had also voted for the new Screamin' Sheiks as a mascot. The red screaming figure with his large mustache, box cutter, and towel thing on his head was much more frightening than the old cartoonish Blue Devil, and it made the school feel multicultural. It was a shame that they had to refinish the entire gym floor.

She walked over to a folding table where a man sat with a laptop.

"Hello," she said.

"Here to vote?" he said.

"I think so," she said. "The nice man out there gave me this piece of paper, is it alright if I bring it?"

"Shouldn't be a problem," said the man. "May I check your driver's license against the rolls? Not that you have to show me your license, you could just tell me your name."

"I don't mind," she said, as she fished her license out of her purse.

"Perfect," he said. After a few moments of inputting her information into the laptop, he walked her over to the voting machine. "Have you ever used one of these?"

"I don't think so," she said.

"Nothing to panic over," he said, sounding more condescending than comforting. "Just use your finger or the stylus, tap on the candidate, and confirm following the prompts, okay?"

"Sure," she said. "Do you mind staying here to make sure I have the hang of it."

"I can't," he said. "Election judges aren't allowed. But, if you have any trouble, I'll just be over there."

"Thank you," she said.

She looked at the screen, and following directions she tapped the banner that read, "TAP HERE TO BEGIN".

The screen swirled in a cacophony of rainbows. She blinked. Hoping that if she did her eyes might refocus on the screen. Letters danced across screen. She looked away and focused on the spot where the Screamin' Sheik. As she took a deep breath the world seemed to calm down.

It's okay. Everything is going to be okay. I'm not broken.

She looked back at the screen. The letters melted into words, and in the upper right hand corner was the face of Jesus. He smiled at her.

She moved her finger toward the smiling face of Jesus. The closer it came the more elated Jesus looked. As she touched the face of Jesus, his eyes rolled into the back of his head, and he disappeared.

As the next screen came into focus she searched quickly to see if Jesus was still there. He was on the bottom left of the screen. She moved her finger away from Jesus, and he looked sad. She stopped and moved it closer and he looked happy again.

As her finger got closer he looked ecstatic.

As she touched him, he moaned and disappeared.

She giggled.

The next screen he looked at her with eyes that danced.

She touched him, and he shivered with excitement.

Each screen she would hunt for the new Jesus. Each page he looked more excited. She liked this Jesus.

Each touch bringing him closer and closer.

As she tapped the last screen and Jesus orgasmed.

Her face was flush.

"That was easy, wasn't it?" said the election judge.

"Ma'am!" said a nervous looking gentleman who was walking toward her across the gym.

Isobel recognized him as the Principal of the elementary school. The slight man walked with an absurd urgency. His shoes squeaking across the newly refinished floor.

"Ma'am," said the Principal, "I thought we talked about this the last time you came on campus."

"I just voted," said Isobel.

"I applaud your civic mindedness," said the Principal, as he began escorting her out of the gym. Isobel wanted to talk the election judge about Jesus on the touch screen.

What a fantastic way to keep voting entertaining!

"There are plenty of other places you could go to vote," continued the Principal, as they began walking toward the parking lot.

"Is this about when I hit the speed bump?" said Isobel. I'm sorry, I didn't mean to be driving that fast, but I needed to get here quickly."

"Why was that?"

"The cupcakes!" said Isobel. "I forgot about the cupcakes."

"What are the cupcakes for, Isobel?"

"The birthday party," said Isobel.

"Who's birthday party?" said the principal. "Can you remember who they're for?"

"My child," said Isobel.

"Can you picture your child?" said the principal.

"Of course I can," said Isobel.

"Tell me about your child, then."

"Umm."

"Let's start with something simple," he said. "Is your child a boy or a girl?"

Isobel thought. She couldn't remember. She knew she had children, but right now she couldn't picture them.

"Now," he continued, "I'm going to have to call your husband."

"I just brought cupcakes," she said. "Please don't call him."

"You asked me, too," he said. "I know you have trouble with your memory, and after everything that you've been through, I want to help. Lat time this happened we discussed what would be best, calling the police or your husband. We decided that calling your husband would be best."

"It's just cupcakes," said Isobel. "They forgot the special order. I asked for enough vegan ones, but they just didn't have them. I'm not exactly sure how many I grabbed, or what kind. She was just so mean."

"Maybe you should wait here while I give him a call."

Isobel knew that would be a very bad idea.

six : the phone is ringing

Isobel opened her eyes. The room had more wood paneling than seemed reasonable. Not that a substantive reduction in wood paneling would make the room look less dated. A velveteen painting of the state of Florida which included an expanded section devoted to the attractions around Sugar Bay County, made certain of that. Isobel couldn't remember spending much time in Sugar Bay County, but knew that the painting's enthusiasm was very optimistic. She was doubtful of the crowds that the Museum of Taxidermic Oddities or the World's Second smallest Post Office could attract. But, she did appreciate the painting's earnestness. Isobel had a soft spot for the roadside attractions that held on, as the looming shadow of Orlando became longer, darker, and more difficult to avoid.

She had always meant to visit that house in Gainesville, the one with all the writing on the walls. Then there was Al's Gator World, Isobel loved going on field trips to Al's Gator World. Margaret, the popular girl in second grade, did nothing but complain that they weren't going someplace cooler. And by cooler she clearly meant somewhere in Orlando.

"The resort we stayed at even let us get into the park a full half hour earlier than everyone else," said Margaret, loud enough for the rest of the bus to hear. "We were the first in line for everything."

"How could you have been first in line for everything?" said Michael Skrugg. "There would have had to be something you weren't first in line for."

"Nobody cares what you think, Michael Skrugg," said Margaret.

Margaret didn't like that Michael had been ignoring her.

Isobel wondered why Margaret tried so hard to be just like the girl in that show.

Isobel tried to remember the name of the show. Every time she felt she had it, it disappeared. She could even see the shape of the letters as they came up on the screen. Isobel could remember sitting in front of the television and sounding out the words. She could see the blond girl on the show the one that no one liked. Everyone could see her schemes coalescing into plot points and lessons for the main character. Isobel wondered why no one else could see it, and stop her. Eventually she understood the reason why no one else saw it was so that the main character in the show could learn something.

Isobel liked to imagine that she was the main character, the one with the long braids in her hair who came running down the hill during the opening credits. If she was the main character then Margaret's random acts had value as lesson for the viewers.

Isobel liked the idea of her pain serving a wider purpose.

Michael Skugg sneezed.

"Bless you," said Isobel.

She felt someone yank her hair. Isobel didn't have to turn around she knew that it had been Margaret. She had done it so viscously, it strained Isobel's neck.

Isobel looked to see if any of the chaperones had seen, as her eyes filled with tears.

"What are you looking for freak?" said Margaret.

"Thank you," said Michael Skrugg.

"Don't mention it," said Margaret. "I'll call her a freak all day long."

"I wasn't talking to you," said Michael Skrugg. "I was talking to Isobel."

"You're welcome," said Isobel. As she felt her face flush, she couldn't fight back a smile.

She knew that Margaret would to make her life miserable, but no matter how hard she tried Margaret couldn't ruin the magic that was Al's Gator World.

Isobel wondered why she could remember this, but had so much difficulty with everything else. Was there a reason? Meaning?

Isobel moved to get up and the figure next to her stirred. Isobel froze.

Had it all been a dream? Who was lying next to her? Was it the faceless man she assumed was her husband, or her new best friend?

Isobel stole a quick glance and was filled with terror. She didn't see Vincent's wig, just the boring short hair of a man.

What if he took it off? It could have fallen off. Don't panic. If it isn't Vincent you can deal with it. You did before and you will again.

Isobel slowly got out of bed and looked at the wiry man in the halter top, and was relived. Outside of the rhythmic breathing of her new best friend the room was still. Not in a frozen claustrophobic kind of way.

Isobel hated that kind of still. That was the kind of still where you woke up in the middle of the night because the covers were too heavy. Where night closed in on you and made it hard to breathe. Searching for any sign of life you get out of bed and wander out of your bedroom and into the long hallway that never seemed to end in your nightmares. Just stretching on and on and on and on and on. You try to not run down the hallway in a panic for fear of waking anyone, because although you're terrified that the whole world has stopped the last thing you want to deal with is having to explain to anyone what is "wrong" with you.

Why can't there be something wrong with the night? The oppressive, unrelenting blackness that is so very terrifying, and so very familiar.

Eventually, you reach the stairs, and somehow you stop shaking long enough to walk down the stairs without slipping and reach the living room. Looking out on the front lawn there is no life. The rabbits that were a menace had been caught and euthanized by the home owners association. The lawns treated with a chemical to discourage their return from areas outside the exclusive gated community. No cars drove through between the hours of two and four a.m., a stipulation put in place to make it easier to spot people who were, "up to no good." Isobel would stand in the living room, trying to find some sign of life outside the stillness.

Anything to assure her that the rest of the world still existed.

That there might possibly be somewhere else to go.

No.

This was not that kind of stillness. This was the kind where it is too early in the morning for anything bad to actually happen. The magical time of early morning, where all of the sins from before pause.

Not for long.

Just for a brief moment of weightlessness, where the world is full of hope and possibility before yesterday can bleed into today, staining it. Insuring that the fresh day not walk away unsullied by its past.

This was that moment magical stillness, before the day could be marred by yesterday.

Isobel removed the velveteen picture from the wall and walked over to the wide picture window that sat above an oversized air conditioner and peeked out through the curtains. The motel sat across the street from a field that was clothed in wisps of mist that would begin to burn off as the sun marched further into the sky.

A slight breeze disturbed the mist. It swirled out of the way and then filled back in behind, not read to forgive its grasp. Isobel loved the way it danced.

It's dancing with me.

She envisioned herself floating with the mist. Swooping close to the ground, narrowly missing it and climbing back into the air. Spinning as a truck rumbled past, faster and faster, then gently slowing, and continuing.

She smiled and tried to get a closer look at the painting.

The phone rang.

Isobel looked at the phone on the end table next to the bed.

The phone rang.

It wasn't that phone. It was a phone outside. Isobel quietly opened the door to the room. She placed one tentative foot out on the cold concrete walkway. The SUV was just to her left. The ringing came from the opposite direction, away from the reception desk. She was happy she didn't have to go toward the old man at the reception desk.

The phone rang

"All I've got is a single," said the old man at the reception desk. He had looked annoyed that someone had woken him when Isobel and Vincent first arrived.

"At this time of night in the middle of fuck nowhere Florida, all you have is a single?" said Vincent. "Convention in town?"

"You don't want the room, fine, I'll head back to bed," said the man.

"No," said Isobel. "We want the room. I could use a nap."

"Sure you could," he said with a creepy smile. "Room's fifty a night, with a refundable deposit for making sure you don't trash the room of another fifty."

"All we're going to do is sleep," said Isobel, as she handed him the credit card.

"Oh, and it's a non-smoking room," he said.

"That's fine," said Isobel. "I tried it a couple of miles back. Didn't care for it."

The phone rang.

Isobel passed the other cars parked outside of the other rooms of the motel. She walked carefully, her bare feet now accustomed to the early morning concrete. She didn't want to get further from Vincent, but she had to answer the phone. She could go back and wake him, but she might miss the call. She couldn't miss the call. What would happen if she did? If she just walked away, what would be the worst that could happen? But, what if it was an emergency? Shouldn't she find someone and tell them? But, what if it was him?

The phone rang

Isobel knelt before the piece of wood. That was all it was, a piece of wood. She was certain if she were to take it down off the wall that she could find where it said, "made in China" on it. She loved the idea of lots of people in China making pewter hippies to nail to pieces of wood. She wondered if any of them actually cared what they were making. If they would rather be making smart phones.

Do they get paid the same? It probably takes a lot more skill to make a smartphone than pewter hippies, but since they're communists do they get paid the same? Which is more boring? With the different things that a smartphone can do, along with upgrades, and different sizes, you're technically making a new phone every few years. But with a pewter hippie aren't you just making the same thing over and over again? Sure, occasionally you get to change up the pewter hippie, going with a hippie for different ethnicity, or changing materials. But, at it's core it is still the same hippie nailed to the same piece of wood.

Her therapist had told her to tell her husband when things got strange. She assumed that orgasming Jesus would be one of those things. So, she told him as soon as she got home.

"What the fuck are you talking about?" said the faceless man. "You don't get to blaspheme like that in my house!"

"I was just telling you what happened," she said. "I was voting and he got his seed all over me. I thought you might be pleased."

"You and those fucking pills!" said the faceless man. "They make you do things you don't mean to, they make you see things that aren't there. You understand that don't you?"

"Why do you get to talk to Jesus, but I don't?"

"What the hell do you mean?"

"Well, you say that you have a good relationship with Jesus," said Isobel. "Maybe this is just my way of putting together a new relationship with him."

"With blasphemy and back talk!"

"No," she said. "Let me explain."

"It is better to live in a corner of a roof, than in a house shared by a contentious woman," said the faceless man.

"No, that isn't what I-"

"It is better to live in a desert land, than with a contentious and vexing woman," he continued. "Go upstairs, and pray on this."

So, she did.

She knelt before the piece of wood.

But, why? It's just a piece of wood. How could a piece of wood be closer to God than his semen?

She turned away from the piece of wood and sat on the kneeler.

I don't like this memory at all. What am I doing now?

The phone rang

She passed the doors to the other rooms until she got to the end of the building. The walkway ended at a drainage ditch that ran along side the motel. Peered down along the drainage ditch she saw an abandoned telephone booth. Isobel couldn't remember the last time she had seen a telephone booth. It sat cockeyed along the bottom of the ditch. Isobel was certain one time the telephone booth had been all shiny chrome and glass, but the years of neglect hadn't been kind to it. Both graffiti and rust had taken their toll.

Maybe, that's what age is, graffiti and rust. People leaving their marks on you, and time eating you away.

The phone rang.

Isobel was happy she hadn't slipped into another memory and stepped of the sidewalk and began walking toward the telephone booth. The ground was frustratingly uneven. Cinder blocks and old pieces of concrete had been dumped into the ditch along with the phone booth. Her bare feet had to angled themselves to grip the debris. She had to check her balance with each step.

"Check you, Cindy Lou," said Vincent. "Pretending to be the man of steel?"

Isobel nearly fell from the shock of hearing Vincent's voice. She turned carefully and waved.

"I was thinking that a cup of coffee and some fresh clothes might just do us both wonders," he continued. "How does that sound to you?"

Isobel turned back to the phone booth.

"It was ringing," said Isobel.

"Okay," said Vincent. "That doesn't mean that it was for you does it? If someone was trying to get in touch with you, wouldn't it be easier to call your cell?"

Isobel took out her phone.

"Do you want to take a picture of the phone booth?"

"Should I?" said Isobel.

"Will it make you feel any better?"

"I don't think so," she said. "But, it might."

"Then take it sweetheart, and then let's find coffee and fresh clothes," said Vincent.

Isobel liked how he made things better, in a way that only a best friend could.

Isobel balanced the coffee between her legs as she pulled into the parking lot of the Hyper-Mart, and weaved around tired shoppers and abandoned carts filled with discarded wrappers, coffee cups, and baby wipes.

A steady stream of angry people dragged bored children toward the entrance. Disappearing as they were gobbled up by the automatic doors. Later they would be spit out with carts laden with their new treasures. Isobel noticed that they looked neither happier, nor relived that they had survived the experience.

"Are you sure this is where you want to go?" said Isobel.

"Nope, but right now our options are limited, and this halter top has seen better days," said Vincent. "All we're looking for is something to change into, a few pairs of underwear, and socks. And if it can be something cute, all the better."

"I guess I didn't plan very well for the trip," said Isobel, as she looked at her outfit. Isobel thought about explaining how these few items had been the only ones not covered in blood, but she wasn't certain if Vincent might admonish her for her lack of planning.

"Oh, I'm not criticizing," said Vincent. "I'm trying to talk myself into it. I can count the number of times I've been into a Hyper-Mart on one hand, and none of them have been a positive experience. The sooner we get in there the sooner we can get out."

Isobel pulled into a parking space next to a cart corral.

"I think I'm ready," she said.

"Hey," said Vincent. "It's going to be alright, I promise. Do you want me to hold your hand?"

"I think I would like that very much, thank you."

Holding Vincent's hand she felt stronger. Like everything that she had to keep at bay inside here wasn't going to explode out in a fountain of lava and terror. It was all manageable. It was all going to be okay.

"You're going the wrong way," said the elderly man, as he shoved his cart through the automatic sliding glass doors.

"Excuse me?" said Isobel.

"The door is clearly marked exit!" he grumbled.

"Does it matter?" said Isobel.

"If they took the time to label the door, why wouldn't you pay attention? It doesn't take that long to read something, does it?"

"I'm sorry," said Isobel.

"Sweetheart," said Vincent, as he rubbed her arm in a comforting way, "there is no reason to engage with the natives."

"What the hell are you supposed to be," he said. "It ain't halloween yet."

Vincent stared down at the the slight aging man.

"There are four things in this world that you can't fix sweetheart," said Vincent. "Stupid, crazy, Nazis, and khakis. Don't waste your time."

Vincent pulled her past the man and into the store.

A wall of sound slammed into her. Parents were screaming at their children. Children were screaming at their parents. Shoppers fought with other shoppers over hard won values they had mined from wobbly racks of clothing. Loud speakers in the ceiling that were dedicated to music were constantly interrupted for announcements for price checks, clean ups, special sales, and cary outs.

"Relax," said Vincent, seeing the terror on Isobel's face. "You're camouflaged. You're dressed like them. You walk like them. You can pass as one of them. And really, if they're spending more time looking at you than me, I'm doing something wrong."

Isobel watched a woman smack her child without breaking her stride.

"I don't think I walk like that."

"Would it help if you were to think of it all as just background noise? You know, like if the world were to suddenly turn into a shower of pink paisleys and emojis would you be able to ignore it all and focus in on the rest of the world?"

"I think so," said Isobel, a child shrieked two isles over. "I think I could try."

"So, why don't you think of this, everything except for me and the clothes is just background noise? Give it a try."

Isobel closed her eyes and concentrated. When she opened her eyes the world was muted, from the colors to the sounds, except for Vincent. She smiled at him, as he began hunting through the racks of white and black clothes, surrounded by people in grayscale.

Isobel looked around, until it caught her eye.

The shirt had the most vibrant demon she had ever seen plastered across its front. The demon was red and sinewy, the name of some band was placed above and below the beautiful art. The visceral nature of the image reminded her of herself. How scary she could be.

"I hope you kept the receipt," said the faceless man.

"Why would I have done that?" said Isobel. "It fits perfectly."

She stood in the middle of the bedroom modeling the red dress.

He stood there staring at her.

"It was on sale," she said. "And it is beautiful."

She looked at him. It was the silence that was the most frightening. She never liked how loud he could yell, but at least she could track where he was. She could plot the arch of his anger, until it eventually subsided. But the quiet, she couldn't gauge. She didn't know where he was. She opened her mouth to tell him the story of how she had found the dress, when he struck her.

Isobel held the t-shirt cautiously in her hands, as if cradling an infant. She absentmindedly grabbed a pair of jeans that were roughly her size, while looking for Vincent.

"You realize that it is a kids shirt," said Vincent, once she found him.

Isobel, unsure of how to respond to his criticism, shuffled her feet. She hadn't meant to make him angry.

Vincent touched her cheek. His hands were calloused. She wondered why she hadn't noticed before.

Someone as glamorous as him, his hands should feel like velvet. Maybe we should go for a manicure? Or a pedicure?

Isobel wondered why that itched at back of her head.

"If it's perfect then it shouldn't matter," said Vincent. "Is it perfect?"

Isobel looked at the shirt and something inside her felt just a little bit warmer. She nodded.

"Then you should get a second and a third!" he said with a smile. "Don't forget clean underwear. I saw a plaid skirt that I need to find in my size. I'll see you in a minute."

Isobel was afraid that if she showed how happy she was she might start to glow and float up to the high ceiling and hit her head.

How would he get me down? If I started to float, there's no saying how long I would be up there.

The joy of the shirt and the joy of her new best friend, would feed the floating, and the floating would create even more joy. Which would make her glow. Isobel imagined that she would be like Christmas star rising above the sales floor. She wondered if people would start a religion around her? Would they make little pewter figures of her in China nailed to pieces of wood. Hopefully, they would remember her super amazing t-shirt.

She turned to run back to grab more shirts when she saw the clown.

Isobel wasn't sure if the woman in front of her was actually dressed like a clown, was something she was imagining, or a bit of both. She felt like her brain was having difficulty understanding what she was actually seeing, so to make sense of it all her brain decided she was seeing a circus clown.

The clown white on the woman's face accentuated her already sour expression. There was a melancholy to her, as if you could see how far the woman's life was from where she had once imagined it.

"What the hell are you looking at?" said the clown.

Isobel slowly took her phone out of her pocket. She didn't mean to be making eye contact with the clown, but she couldn't look away.

"What the hell are you doing?"

"Taking your picture to see if you're real," said Isobel, trying to steady her voice.

"The fuck do you mean by that?" said the clown.

"Taking a picture helps me. My best friend can tell you. He was here just a minute ago."

"Why the hell wouldn't I be real?" said the clown. "What the is wrong with you? You ask people before you take their fucking picture!"

"May I take your picture?"

"Hell no!"

Isobel was surprised how the clown kept swearing.

I wouldn't hire her for my kids party.

Not that Isobel would hire a clown for a party, she found them creepy.

A small crowd began to gather sneaking peeks of what was happening. They weren't brazen enough to gawk, they casually inspected tags on clothing, close to, but not right next to, the unfolding drama. They wanted to see what was happening, but didn't want to get involved.

"Sorry, I didn't mean to offend you," said Isobel. "I have difficulties sometimes. Figuring out what's real and what isn't. My therapist suggested I take a picture when I get confused. Not the therapist that wanted to have sex with me, the new one that always seems bored. I just want to see if you're a clown, or if I'm just making it all up in my head."

"You want to see if I'm a fucking clown? Jesus, what the fucking hell is wrong with you, fucking freak!"

Isobel melted away from the crowd and sank into the middle of a large circular clothing rack and closed her eyes.

"What the hell is she doing?" said the clown.

"Is she hiding from you?" said a new voice.

"Jesus," said the clown, "somebody get a manager, I think she's tweaking."

"She has to be on something," said another voice. "Did you see how crazy she looked?

Isobel liked how the voices became muffled by the clothes, as she sank into the middle of the large round rack. If she sat her long enough, she wondered, will all melt into nothing?

How will Vincent find me?

"Isobel?" called Vincent's muffled voice from the other side of the rack. "Isobel? Are you alright?"

"I don't think I am," said Isobel, as she exited the rack and walked into Vincent. "Unless we're leaving."

"I think we can," he said. "Do you still have your shirts?"

Isobel looked at the shirt in her hand and smiled. It was so beautiful.

"Yes," she said, trying to sound brave. "I also have a pair of jeans, and some underwear and socks."

"Did you get the underwear in the kids department, or did you actually get something that will fit?"

"I think they'll fit," she said. "I think I may need some new shoes as well."

Isobel thought about how much fun it was going to be once they reached the frontier. They could make their own clothes instead of having to come to places like this. Of course, they would have to learn how to make clothes, but that couldn't be too hard. She remembered seeing something about how kids could be taught to make sneakers and other articles of clothing. If a kid could do it she should be able to do it too.

"We can head to the shoe department," said Vincent.

"No," said Isobel. "Please, we need to leave."

"If have to go somewhere else for shoes, we have to go somewhere else for shoes," said Vincent.

Isobel smiled and held his hand. She knew nothing bad could happen to her if she was holding her best friend's hand.

"Let's go check out," he continued. "If we use the self checkout we don't even have to talk to anyone."

"Does it have a touch screen?"

"I think so," he said. "Is that alright?"

"I might need some help," said Isobel. "I have trouble with touch screens."

"Do they give you a headache?"

"No, I see Jesus in them."

"Does he tell you to do things?" he said.

"No, I poke him until he comes."

"Oh."

"There she is!" cried out the clown.

Isobel gipped Vincent's hand tighter. The clown came running with a security guard.

"Hello," said Vincent. "How may I help you?"

"Fuck," said the clown. "You're just as much a freak as she fucking is."

Isobel fought the urge to hurt her. How dare she talk to her best friend like that.

"Is there a problem?" said Vincent to the security guard, purposely ignoring the clown.

"She tried to take a picture of me," said the clown. "Then she hid in a rack of clothing."

"Maybe it was because she was frightened by the way you're raising your voice," said Vincent.

"Who the fuck do you think you are to blame me for her being a fucking whack job?"

"Alright," said Vincent, "I'm assuming that you're going to ask us to leave."

"I actually wasn't sure," said the security guard. "She just made me come over."

"I understand," said Vincent. "We were just heading to the check out."

"You didn't answer my fucking question," said the clown.

"Ma'am," said Vincent, "I'm really not invested in this conversation at all. If you want to take away the idea that my friend and I are in the wrong, fine."

Isobel felt her face flush.

Did he really just call me his friend? Don't float, not now!

"You want me to be the asshole in all of this," continued Vincent, "fine. I really don't care, as long as this interaction can be over."

Vincent turned to Isobel and smiled.

Isobel felt so light she might not need shoes.

seven : glorp

Isobel stood at the entrance to the mall. Black tinted doors stood at the end of a concrete corridor that lead off the massive, yet empty parking lot. Along the walls of the manufactured valley were posters of people enjoying themselves. A pair of women laughed while they clutched each other's arms, their eyes betraying the staged moment. Isobel wondered why they never bothered to alter the eye, or give the models sunglasses to hide how much they were lying. Isobel knew that you can't fake emotions with your eyes. People can smile, but their eyes can't hide how sad they are.

"Why do they do that?" said Isobel, as she stood closer to Vincent.

"Do what?" said Vincent.

"The pictures," said Isobel, "It is a manufactured lie. There won't be a single person in there that is anywhere near as happy as the models in those pictures."

"Sweetheart," said Vincent, "have you ever eaten a burger from a fast food joint?"

"Of course," said Isobel.

"Did it ever taste as good as they made it look in the commercials?" said Vincent. "You know that moment of ecstasy like it is the best thing they've ever eaten."

"No," said Isobel. "Usually, they give me a headache and diarrhea."

"Exactly," said Vincent. "If they put that on the commercial, no one would ever eat a burger, and we'd be overrun by cattle."

"But, that's a commercial."

"Just because you don't have your ass glued to your couch, sweetheart, doesn't mean that it isn't all one big fat commercial," said Vincent.

"I don't know," said Isobel. "It just feels wrong."

"It's a mall," he said. "If it didn't feel a little bit wrong, you're not doing it right."

Vincent strode up to the glass door and said, "The sooner we get in, the sooner we get to leave."

Isobel walked past him into the cavernous mall. Her footfalls on the brown linoleum echoing through the vast space. High above them skylights that once allowed natural light into the mall were now covered in dust and grime, creating shadows where none had been designed to be. A line of empty store fronts had metal grates pulled down over them, protecting the handful of shoppers from the scattered remains littering the scarce interiors of shuttered stores. Muzak faintly played a familiar tune through broken speakers. Isobel had enjoyed the song High School, but couldn't remember who sung it. She knew it was a sad song that bemoaned the tragic sameness of suburban America. She wondered if it was meant to be ironic?

"Where is everyone?" said Isobel.

"Staying away, because they don't like the marketing either. Come on."

"What about the zombies?"

"Why?" said Vincent. "Have you seen any?"

"No, but there was this movie," said Isobel. "They were in this abandoned mall, and were trying to keep the zombies out. They were trying to find supplies, and they did! But, then there were all the zombies. They also had a helicopter on the roof and blocked the doors with giant trucks."

"Well, we don't have a helicopter, or trucks, but we are here for supplies," said Vincent. "What do you think the number one thing you'll probably need in case of zombies?"

"A gun," said Isobel. "But, I don't think they have a gun store in here. Is that what they call it a gun store? You know what I mean? Like how you get food at a grocery store, or hats at a haberdashery? Is there a special term for a gun store?"

"Do, I come across as the type a person who might know?" said Vincent.

"No, but you do seem very smart," said Isobel.

"Here I thought you were going one way, and you zagged another and turned it into a compliment," said Vincent. "Sweetheart, I was talking about shoes you can run in. In all of those movies, eventually they run out of bullets and gas. If they had invested in functional, yet fashionable footwear they could have made it."

I chose the right best friend.

"As far as what a gun store is called," continued Vincent, "I don't know."

With the right pair of running shoes I can out run faster than the zombies, and everything else!

She looked down at the black ribbon that whirred below her pounding feet. As her foot struck the tread it flexed slightly and sprang back again. She knew that every foot fall, every stride, every minute spent on the treadmill would get her closer to where she needed to be.

Where he said she should be.

Further from where she was.

This would make her better.

He would look at her with something other than condescension and appeasement.

He would stop trying to calm her down. He would stop taking all of her anger and frustration. He would understand that she was strong enough to wield it herself.

I can show him how much I can do. If I spend long enough on the treadmill I can be everything.

She pressed the button that made it go faster, the one that made her better even faster.

"I was good at running," said Isobel.

"Let's see what they have at the Circus of Shoes," said Vincent

Isobel never liked shoe stores.

Some stores openly cater to a specific gender. Others to a specific style or ascetic. But, regardless most stores would have a plethora of sizes, styles, and patterns. Shoe stores reduce people to their basest demographic profile. Hurtful assumptions are extracted from this data and masculine and feminine are defined and segregated. Shoes in pink and pastel hues are relegated to the women's section, work boots hidden in the men's.

What if Isobel wanted to get steel toe work boots in her size? What if a man with size fourteen feet wanted to get the same work boots in cherry apple red with a six inch heel? Choices of what is socially acceptable are made for you. Basketball shoes, with the names of male players emblazoned on their sides, littered the boy's department. A meger handful of the same shoes marketed by the same male athletes, but in pastel, could be found in the girls section.

This was why Isobel was surprised when she walked into Circus of Shoes. It looked as if a bored child had tried to arrange the shoes by color, got bored and tried grouping them by size; eventually giving up and shoved as many on the shelves as could fit.

"Hello and welcome to Circus of Shoes, where we aren't clowning around on the prices," said a bored, young woman.

"That's better," said the young man next to her. "But, next time it would be better if you didn't do it in such a monotone."

"Fuck, Jimmy," said the young woman, "these are the first customers we've had all week."

"You're not counting the homeless guy who stopped in to ask for change, and free shoes," said the young man named Jimmy.

"I don't see the point in any of this," said the first teenager.

"You're doing great," said Jimmy. "We've got an entire month for you to turn it around, and then Mr. Zymanski will be sure to write you a letter of recommendation."

"I don't know," said the young woman named Sally.

"Trust me," said Jimmy to Sally, before turning his attention back to Isobel. "Sorry, with the store closing Sally asked me to coach her. Everyone is applying to work at the HyperMart. Any edge you can get helps."

"Sorry the store is closing," said Isobel.

"Why?" said Sally.

"With how dead the mall has been, it's beginning to feel like that horror movie," said Jimmy.

"That's what I was telling him!" said Isobel. "It is scary."

"I know, right?" said Jimmy. "No one comes to the mall anymore. They've even brought in a carnival to try to remind people that the mall is here before the holidays. Now, what can we help you find, that you couldn't find at the HyperMart?"

"Or online?" said Sally.

"I need a pair of solid running shoes," said Isobel. "And Vincent needs something fabulous in a women's size-"

"Fifteen," said Vincent.

"Wow," said Jimmy, locking eyes with Vincent. "You are gorgeous!" Jimmy's face flashed bright red, as he looked away. Vincent looked aloof, but his eyes danced.

"Do you remember that shipment of off sized rollie shoes that Mr. Zymanski was loosing his mind over last week?" said Sally, trying to help Jimmy. "Why don't I show her the running shoes, and you can take him, wait, forgive my ignorance. Do you prefer gender neutral pronouns? I have a friend that prefers gender neutral pronouns. I'm practiced at them, I'm just not sure what's the right way to ask."

"Do you think I spend this much fucking time on my makeup to be 'gender neutral'?"

"Sorry," said Sally.

"Vincent prefers male pronouns," said Isobel.

"That was yesterday," said Vincent. "Now, where are these shoes?"

"There in the back," said Jimmy. "Do you want to wait here?"

"Why don't you have him head back there with you?" said Sally. "Don't worry, I've got everything out here."

"Umm," said Jimmy. "I'm not sure that Mr. Zymanski would be alright with that."

"Then I'll be sure not to tell him," said Sally.

"In that case," said Vincent, "lead on."

Jimmy tripped, caught himself, and fell through the door that lead to the stock room. Vincent reflexively smiled at how sweet Jimmy seemed, and followed him.

"I think your friend is a real inspiration," said Sally, as she walked Isobel toward the running shoes.

"He's my best friend," said Isobel.

"Have you known each other long?" said Sally.

"No," said Sally. "But, I feel like everything started when we first met. Like everything that came before right now, wasn't really me. Like watching T.V., you can see where it's all going, but no matter how loud you scream, it all keeps getting away from you. But when Vincent showed up, I was able to get up from the couch and begin to live a new life. Do you know what I mean?"

"I don't," said Sally. "But, I think it is sweet. What do you usually wear in an athletic shoe?"

"I don't remember," said Isobel. "I'm sorry."

"That's alright," said Sally. "Let's have some fun."

"I don't think I'm having fun anymore," she said. She liked how the cool bathroom tile felt against her cheek, until she saw how much dust had accumulated behind the toilet.

How could that much dust settle behind there? Where did it come from?

"Damnit, why do you have to push like this?" said her Husband. "You know this is where it leads."

She turned and tried to look at his face, but it was the same featureless flesh colored oval.

Strange, you live with someone for that long, and they have such an impact on your life, but at a moment like this I still can't remember what he looks like?

"Get back to bed!" he screamed at a small figure appearing behind him.

"Stop!" she said. "I hate it when you talk to him like that."

"I don't get to say a whole hell of a lot at the moment," he said. "Do you? I mean is this really how your brain is wired, or are you just stupid? I'm standing here trying to knock some sense into you, and you just keep pushing."

"Please stop," she said.

"No, this is all on you," he said.

"Please, I don't want to do this anymore," she said, as she stood up.

"This is what you told me to do," he said. "You said this was what you needed to get your head right again."

"No, I think I've had enough," she said.

"What?" he said, as he moved to slap her hard across the face with the back of his hand.

She waited for the pain, but instead his hand passed through her head. She could remember the pain the first time she lived through this, so why bother experiencing it again if this is only a memory?

He continued to scream at her, so she muted him like he was a loud and annoying commercial for an auto dealership.

His arms flailed around silently. Isobel smiled at how comical his gestures were. She wondered how she ever found him frightening?

She tried her hardest to remember his face.

The flesh colored oval shifted and features began to take shape.

Her husband swung wildly at her again, his fists passing directly through her.

She shifted to get a good look at the emerging face, and saw a bloody visage with dead eyes. She stopped trying to remember and it swirled back to the featureless flesh colored oval.

That's better.

Shrugging off the specter that continued to kick and scream where she once had been, she walked out of the bedroom, past the piece of wood on the wall, and toward the winding staircase. Walking past the little boy's bedroom, stoping in front of the door at the top of the stairs.

What is in there?

Why couldn't she remember what was behind the door? She willed herself to walk toward it. Her legs felt like lead. She tried to reach her arm out to grab the door handle, but she was frozen in terror. Why was she so afraid to find what was behind the door?

"How do those fit?" said Sally.

Isobel looked down at her feet and saw the most beautiful pair of red sneakers she had ever seen. She loved how new and beautiful her world was. She began to tear up.

"Oh, if they aren't right, I am so sorry," said Sally, "we can try another pair."

"No," said Isobel, wiping the tears away and smiling, "they're perfect. Besides red shoes are faster."

"Do you want to give them a quick try?" said Sally.

"Can I?" said Isobel.

"Why not? The mall is empty. It's always fucking empty."

Isobel smiled at Sally. She liked Sally. Isobel thought about talking to Vincent to see if inviting Sally to join them in the frontier would be a good idea? Vincent would know.

Isobel walked out into the empty mall. She stretched for a brief moment, then began to jog slowly across the brown linoleum tile, past the beige walls and empty store fronts. Behind her a department store that dominated one end of the mall became smaller and smaller. Her feet gained momentum as she followed a bend in the walkway. She ran past a dry fountain and an abandoned food court. She looked down and saw her feet becoming a red blur against the brown.

Then she saw the zombie.

It was behind a display window in one of the empty store fronts. Isobel thought about pulling out her phone to see if it was her mind playing tricks on her. But, whenever anyone stopped in those movies to see if what they were seeing was actually a zombie, that would be when another zombie would jump out of nowhere and attack the person. She wasn't going to let herself be victimized. Not anymore. Not now that she had found her best friend. Everything was different now.

She was brand new.

Shinny.

Beautiful.

She was no longer bruised. She wasn't even smudged.

She continued running, circling back, past the window with the zombie and back around the bend. As Isobel drew closer, she saw the most beautiful thing she had ever seen, Vincent roller skating in front of the Circus of Shoes.

"What do you think?" he said, as he spun like a ballerina.

"I think you're amazing," said Isobel.

"So, do I," said Jimmy, as he blushed, again.

"Jimmy is going to be too shy to ask you both, but would you like to go to the carnival tonight?" said Sally. "It is nothing big, a few rides and a haunted house, just outside in the mall parking lot."

"Is Jimmy asking me out on a date?" said Vincent.

"It doesn't have to be," said Jimmy.

"What if I want it to be?" said Vincent.

Jimmy tried to hide his smile.

"The four of us could grab a bite before," said Sally. "Jimmy will be much to shy to speak unless I'm there."

"Sounds wonderful," said Vincent, as he skated circles around Jimmy.

Isobel thought he looked like a figure skater. She envied his confidence. Vincent skated toward the exit, smiling back at Jimmy.

"Don't panic," said Vincent.

"Why would I panic?" said Isobel, as she held the door for Vincent to exit the mall. The change from the temperature controlled mall, to the Florida heat was more of a shock than usual. Isobel began to sweat, but shivered as a blast of air conditioned air swept past them.

"Because, we need to find something to wear for tonight," said Vincent.

"We just picked up all of those clothes from the HyperMart."

"Dear, if you think for one moment that I am planning on corrupting that young man in a wardrobe we picked from the bargain racks at a fucking HyperMart you are sorely mistaken," said Vincent.

"Oh," said Isobel, "I'm sorry, I didn't know."

"Dear, there are going to be volumes written about what you didn't know before you were lucky enough to find me," said Vincent. "But, don't worry, I'll be gentle."

"I didn't think you wouldn't be," said Isobel. "I mean why would you hurt me?"

"Exactly," said Vincent, "I'm just here to make you better."

She found it hard to breathe in the steam. She didn't know why she couldn't catch her breath. She moved to turn off the water in the shower, and a hand slapped her away.

"No," he said. "You, don't get to touch that."

"I can't breathe," she said.

"If you can't breathe you can't talk," he said. "How are you talking right now if you can't breathe?"

"Please," she said. "I can't catch my breath."

"What did I just say?" he said. "Do you want me to turn it colder?"

"Yes, please," she said.

A hand reached in past the shower curtain, and turned off the hot water.

Why would a husband do this?

The heat vanished from the water, but the freezing cold water bit at her flesh. She recoiled. The steam dissipated. She took a deep cleansing breath, then faced the water defiantly. It was nothing but water. It couldn't beat her, no matter how long he made her stand in it.

He was muttering something abusive. She could make out the words, "whore" and "bitch" but the rest was lost. It followed the water down the drain. She urinated, allowing her warm piss to run down her legs and over all of his words.

"What the hell do you think you're doing?" he said.

"Peeing," she said, clenching her jaw, knowing what was coming.

"That's disgusting," he said after he struck her. From the way the faceless man winced she knew it hurt his hand. That made her proud.

"You do the same thing," she said, "every morning."

"That's different."

"Why?"

"What has gotten into you?" he said. "What makes you think you can talk to me like that?"

I'm your wife, not your child.

She wasn't certain if she said it, or only thought it. The world irised to black.

The department store was dated, the women's section even more so. Orange carpets collected dust under round displays of clothing that seamlessly meandered between hooker chic and Florida Grandmother. One shirt bridged both with sparkle bubble letters that stated, "GMILF".

The few employees crowded around a cracked make-up counter and mumbled in the general direction of the rare sighting of an actual customer. Vincent and Isobel had found the lone three way mirror across from the restrooms on the opposite side of the store from the actual dressing rooms. Isobel sat on the brown vinyl cube that had been the store's poor excuse of a guy seat.

"What do you think of this one?" said Vincent, as he tried to angle himself away from the crack in one mirror and the large brown spot on another.

"I think it looks very red," said Isobel. "If I like it, do I have to wear one?"

Vincent was modeling a red vinyl dress. It was tight in a flattering way.

"Why would you wear one?" said Vincent. "Are you trying to impress someone?"

"No," said Isobel. "So, I can wear what I'm wearing now?"

"Why not?" he said. "We're heading to a carnival."

"Thank goodness," said Isobel. "In that case, I like the dress, it is very flattering on you. But, it seems a bit much for the carnival."

"How do you mean a bit much?" said Vincent. "A bit much in an over dressed sense, or in a hooker, stripper kind of way."

"Hooker, stripper," said Isobel.

"I know, but I love the way it fits," said Vincent.

"Is it hard to find things that fit?"

"You have no idea," said Vincent.

"I guess I don't," said Isobel. "I just assumed-"

"What?" said Vincent. "That since I'm a guy I wouldn't be so picky?"

"No," said Isobel. "I was going to say you're so thin I would think that you'd look great in everything."

"Oh," said Vincent. "Again you zag with the compliments."

"Thank you," said Isobel. "I'm just afraid that if you show up dressed in that he might get the wrong idea."

"Tell me dear, what wrong idea is that?"

"That you're only interested in him for one thing, and that you only want him to be interested in you for one thing. Just because I've never enjoyed that one thing, doesn't mean you shouldn't. But, you just seem like there was more there than just that. I mean between you too. I could have imagined it. Like the zombie. But, since I didn't take a picture of it, I don't know."

"Hold on," said Vincent. "What?"

"Well, while I was running I saw this thing in one of the stores," said Isobel.

"No, not that," said Vincent. "You imagined the zombie."

"How do you know?" said Isobel.

"When the zombies first attack everyone runs screaming, right?"

"I guess."

"Do you hear anyone screaming right now?"

Isobel listened to hear if she could. The only thing she could hear was the distant murmur of the people at the cracked make up counter.

"No, I don't," said Isobel.

"See, no screaming, no zombies. Okay?"

Why didn't I think of that? I need to stop saying stupid things.

"I don't think I've ever enjoyed sex," she said. "I can't remember a time when I did. Or maybe I don't want to remember what it was like with my husband. I don't want to remember his face. Maybe I don't want to remember sex."

"That is sad," said Vincent, as he removed the dress and began to try on another one.

"I appreciate you wanting to help me."

"I'm going to have to stop you there," said Vincent. "Understand, I am only telling you this because I don't want you to be 'that' girl."

"What girl?" asked Isobel.

"You know, that stereotype," said Vincent. "You know what I mean, please don't make me say it. I've always hated the label."

"I don't kn-"

"Fag hag," said Vincent. "I hate it so much, I didn't want to say it, but sweetheart you have to understand I am not that kind of Queen. This isn't that kind of after school special. The one where I help you blossom into a heathy sexual being, while spewing a few lines of ignorant drivel, for comic relief. All the time ignoring that you have the body of who I assume is your husband in the back of that enormous SUV of yours."

Isobel, began to cry.

"Oh, dear," continued Vincent. "Let's take a deep breath. This isn't anything personal, but I've got enough on my hands trying to navigate my sex life, I have neither the time, nor the energy to help you with yours. I'm certain you are seriously repressed, and once you find what color your parachute is, and let your freak flag fly, you'll have a fantastic time. But, I am not some kind of shaman to show you the way. I'm a quickly aging transvestite who is desperate to find something for him to wear on a date tonight with a very cute, very sweet boy, who may run back into the closet so fast it'll make both our heads spin. So let's focus on the task at hand shall we? I know there must be a lot going on in that head of yours."

"Who are you?" said Isobel.

Vincent looked at her smiled and began to spin. The red dress he was wearing billowing out.

As Isobel watched, the world began to dim around the edges. Isobel looked away and the department store broke apart. Beneath it was a cavernous sound stage. Isobel blinked and realized she was sitting alone in the studio audience. A pair of cameramen wheeled impressive looking cameras across the stage floor in response to orders being barked in their ears through sequined headsets that kept their wigs from moving. Behind her, Isobel could just make out Vincent. He stood before of a bank of monitors in a darkened control room, their light illuminating his face in a much more flattering way then one might assume it would. She moved to come and join him in the booth, but he motioned that she stay where she was.

Slowly the lights in the studio dimmed. Isobel relaxed into her seat. It was surprisingly comfortable. She remembered the last time she had been to see a show and how uncomfortable the seats had been. The lights on the stage floor warmed, revealing a modest middle class ranch home. The aluminum siding was a tastefully faded lime green. A lone palm tree in the front yard grew. As Isobel stared at it, it began to move toward her. Before she had a chance to marvel at how the illusion was managed the front facade of the house folded to the sides. Inside was a familiar looking wood paneled basement. Isobel had never seen it before, but it reminded her so much of every other wood paneled basement she had ever seen, she could imagine the reassuring scent of mildew.

Isobel stole a glance back at at Vincent in the control room. He flashed her a smile that, to her, was everything. She turned back around and a lone spotlight illuminate a lone man sitting on a stool. Isobel's jaw dropped when she realized that the man was Vincent. She turned around to see if he could possibly be in two places at once, but he was gone from the control room.

"You have to understand that there are rules," said Vincent. He exuded a relaxed elegance. Isobel assumed that he must either have been born with it, or must be something he practiced daily. Vincent took a deep breath and continued, "I mention this, not as an some kind of expert, or authority figure, but more so that you can understand the construct of the little world we have created here for you, and establish my contract with you, the audience."

Vincent jumped down from the stool which was now much taller than it had been moments ago. So, tall that Isobel worried for his safety. But he landed on the stage floor, so lightly it was easy to imagine that he had floated for just the split second before he landed.

"I don't want this to start like bad community theatre. I don't want this to start like some self important high school production of with me playing some folksy narrator sitting down stage and constantly commenting on the action behind me. That would be affected and overly staged. But, to be fair, this story has been staged. I point that out, because there will be some that may admonish me for neglecting their parts in this story, or telling it from a point of view that may not jive with their perceived reality. It would be easy to say to them that if they don't like it they are more than welcome to put on their own show. So I will do just that, 'If you don't like this, go put on your own damn show.' That felt better than I expected it to."

Isobel laughed, as she did the sound of dozens of other people laughed as well. Isobel looked around the darkened seats to see if she was still alone. Vincent said something else and the same laughter erupted from the imaginary people around her. Isobel didn't like the canned laughter, it sounded like something out of a nightmare. Turing her attention back to the stage, she saw Vincent sitting naked in-front of a mirror.

"The biggest thing to remember is that all of this is the truth. I promise that I will not lie to you. I do not pretend that you will enjoy my truths, but they are just that."

The sound of polite applause rang in Isobel's ears, as it echoed across the empty chairs.

"All it is is lipstick," said Vincent. "But, even simple lipstick, purchased from a corner drug store, can change everything."

Vincent pulled the top off the lipstick and began applying it. Somehow it effected more than just his lips. It was as if the lipstick were the mere catalyst to allowing him bloom before her very eyes.

"What the hell are you-" said a young man, as he entered through a door. As he slammed it behind him the entire wall of the set wavered. He noticed this and looked behind him nervously. He was visibly uncomfortable, not from finding Vincent, but from being on stage. Even after he assed that the set wasn't going to fall down, he shuffled his feet and swayed slightly as she stole glances at the empty chairs.

"Why, Dad?" said Vincent. "Why can't you accept me for who I am?"

Vincent stood and walked away from the tableau, which had been created from the actor playing "Dad" shuffling and swaying slightly. Isobel could tell that he was supposed to be "frozen" and if he had been it would have completed a striking picture, but instead the nervous energy added to the earnestness of the scene.

"Is this is where I say something cliché?" said Vincent, directly to Isobel. "Possibly. Now, I would never presume that my story is the story of every closeted teenage boy who dreams of performing in drag. There is a common emotional vocabulary to those of us living on the margins. A spiritual regionalism that can develop in the tenor of experience. So, please understand that if you find similarities between my stories and others, it is not me generalizing."

Isobel watched as Vincent turned back to the young man playing his father, and the action resumed.

"This is what I am Dad," said Vincent. "This is what I am!"

"I know son," said the young man. "I have known for so long. I've just been waiting for you to know. And it is-"

The young man froze. He was trying to find the right word, it was there somewhere, but he just couldn't find it.

"Don't ask for your line," said Vincent. "Damnit, how many times have we been over this fucking scene?"

"Beautiful?" he guessed.

"Thank you," said Vincent. "See when you trust it, the word is right there isn't it? It is when you second guess yourself that you lose it. The script makes sense, trust it."

Vincent smiled at the young man who was playing his father. The young man broke character and smiled back.

"What a fun twist isn't it?" said Vincent.

"Yes it is," said Isobel. "I have to say I thought he was going to freak out on you."

"I guess we're all full of surprises aren't we?" said Vincent. "But, no one as much so as my father."

The lights quickly darkened. Isobel could almost see a ghost image of Vincent in the black. Standing where he had been moments before. The sound of movement came from the stage floor. Isobel assumed that they were changing the set, and repositioning the cameras.

In the black Vincent's voice boomed, "He took me to my first drag show. That's the kind of man my father was.

Please, hear and understand the use of the past tense when referring to him. It hearts my heart to say it."

The stage exploded in light and disco music. Men dressed in elaborate gowns danced across the stage.

"Please forgive the stereotype, but it was seventies night," said Vincent who appeared in a corner of the stage with the young man who was playing his father. Dressed in a simple t-shirt and jeans provided a stark contrast to Vincent's yellow sun dress and beehive wig.

"Don't be nervous," said the young man in the same tentative cadence. "You look fantastic."

"Now," said Vincent, as everything paused, "I would never wish the feelings of isolation and fear that I experienced on anyone. I know that I am far from the only one who has ever felt like that. But, this moment right now. The moment of finally finding acceptance for who I am, along with finding other beautiful creatures just like me, and having them welcome me into this community, is a singular bliss that I hope everyone gets an opportunity to experience once in their lives."

The action on the stage continued, as Vincent and the young man playing his father weaved their way through the crowd.

"Here they took me under their wing," said Vincent. "Showing me tips and tricks to makeup, diet, and dating. My dad would bring me at least once a week. How amazing was that? He didn't just drop me off either. He would wait to watch me perform."

Everyone danced to the music, occasionally stopping and creating a tableau. At first the freezing tableau moments seemed arbitrary. But, soon they fell into steady rhythm of beat, freeze, beat, beat, freeze. Isobel felt though that they were beginning to speed up, making her feel more anxious.

"I would like to say that we saw them coming," said Vincent. "That they showed up in pickup trucks and cowboy hats. They were dressed like my dad, and one of them even drove a high end German automobile. The irony of which was not lost on me. The official police report stated that it was one person acting alone. I know it wasn't."

"FAGGOTS!" boomed a chorus of angry voices.

A new group entered the crowd of dancers. They were violent, screaming. Isobel hid behind her chair. She covered her ears, and closed her eyes tight.

A gentle hand touched Isobel's face. She opened her eyes to see Vincent standing before the same mirrors in the department store.

"Who am I?" said Vincent. "This is who I am."

"Thank you," said Isobel. "You're my best friend."

"That is sweet," said Vincent. "But, before we go much further we need to talk about the dead body in your SUV."

"So, it doesn't freak you out that my dead husband is in the car?"

"Not unless you plan on me joining him," said Vincent.

"No, of course not."

"I'm assuming he was a royal fucking waste of oxygen , and deserved it," said Vincent.

"I think so, but I don't remember," said Isobel.

"Did you kill him?"

"I don't remember."

"Well, that's good enough for me!"

"Really?"

"Sure," said Vincent. "However, before we head to meet up with Jimmy, we need to either stash him somewhere, or get some air freshener. He is starting to get a little ripe. I guess I'm that sort of Queen, the kind that helps you dispose of a body."

"Thank you," said Isobel. "What should we do with him?"

"Please stop smiling," said Vincent, as he struggled with the top half of the body.

"Sorry," said Isobel. "I'm not trying to. I'm so happy I might fly away."

They had been lucky when they found the old grease dumpster behind the abandoned restaurant. The faded letters on the front of the building declared that it had been a Pizza place. Isobel thought the stucco building looked more like a Mexican restaurant. When they had first pulled the body from the back of the SUV, Isobel caught a glimpse of her husband's face, and was thankful that she couldn't remember it.

"I'm so lucky that I found you," Isobel continued.

"Nope, we are not having a moment!" said Vincent. "In a minute you are going to open that grease dumpster and we are going to fight the urge to vomit."

"I doubt it smells that bad," said Isobel.

"Have you ever worked in a restaurant?"

"I don't think so."

"Trust me," said Vincent, "this is going to be rough."

Isobel placed her husband's feet down on the black top and ran back to the SUV to grab the bolt cutters and a padlock. As she did, her husband released some gas.

It couldn't smell any worse than that.

She was wrong.

She cut the lock off the dumpster, and lifted the lid slightly, then vomited on her husband's feet.

"I know it smells horrible, but remember it needs to," said Vincent. "If it smells horrible then it will hide the smell of a body. If we work together, we can get this over with and be far, far away."

"Okay," said Isobel, as she took a deep breath and held it.

It took some effort, but as the body slid under the decaying grease with a satisfying, "glorp," Isobel felt like dancing again.

"If you don't stop smiling," said Vincent, as he closed and secured the new padlock to the dumpster, "I am never helping you dispose of another body again."

eight : tilt-a-whirl

Vincent stood in the middle of the empty mall parking lot in a short plaid skirt and white blouse. If his hair had been in a pair of pig tails and had been wearing knee socks he would have looked like the approximation of an overly sexualized school girl as portrayed in a 90's music video. Instead the way that Vincent carried himself, the look was elegant, yet approachable.

"I'm nervous," said Vincent. "Why am I nervous?"

"I don't know?" said Isobel.

"That is not the most supportive thing to say," said Vincent.

"I'm sorry," said Isobel. "I can't remember dating very much."

"Damnit, Izzy," he said. "This is not all about you, okay? What did I say after we got rid of the body?"

"I could let it be about me until you found some hand sanitizer," said Isobel.

"And did we find the hand sanitizer?"

"Yes," said Isobel, proudly. "I had some in the glove box."

"So, now let's focus, it needs to be about me," said Vincent. "I am freaking out and I don't want to hear about how you can't remember being nervous for some generic kid to pick you up for prom. We've got the entire John Hughes catalog to watch if we need to make your gated community upbringing more relatable. I'm dealing with real problems.

What if he doesn't like this look? What if he thinks I look trashy?"

"I don't think you look like a hooker."

"You say the sweetest things, and then you say that," said Vincent. "To be fair, I'm certain your idea of a 'fierce' look is high heels and a smokey eye. I'm trying to create a feeling of, wow."

"Oh," said Isobel. "Okay."

Isobel was so thankful that she had found Vincent, otherwise she might not know about any of these things. There were so many people in the world who weren't as lucky as she was. Who weren't lucky enough to have a best friend. Who didn't have their own Vincent. She was excited about the things he was going to teach her.

"Don't worry," he said. "I don't blame you. It has something to do with cul-de-sacs, in gated communities. They don't let the chi flow. It gets trapped, creating eddies of boredom and privilege."

"Thank you," said Isobel. "You are my best frie-"

"Good evening," interrupted Vincent, as he looked past her.

She turned to see what he was looking at to find Jimmy and Sally walking towards them. Jimmy looked smart in a light blue polo shirt and khaki cargo shorts. Isobel wondered if Vincent would be willing to ignore the cargo shorts.

Or, maybe, he might teach him things too! It will be like Vincent's school! We can learn and grow together once we reach the frontier.

"Wow," said Jimmy. "You look beautiful."

Isobel was so excited for Vincent that he got his, "Wow!" She tried to steal his attention for a moment to tell him, but he wouldn't look at her. Jimmy and Vincent quickly walked ahead, toward the carnival. Isobel tried to make out what they were saying to one another.

"This isn't a double date, right?" said Sally.

Isobel had forgotten about Sally. She was dressed much like Isobel in a simple t-shirt and jeans. Isobel thought about telling her about how the HyperMart had shirts that were much more fun that what she was wearing, but she didn't want Sally to feel bad about her boring t-shirt.

"I didn't think about it," said Isobel. "I don't think this is a double date. Do you want it to be one?"

"No," said Sally. "I'm just fine with us keeping each other company while they make eyes at one another. Jimmy's needed this for a long time. He's been closeted for so long, I was beginning to wonder if he was staying in there because it was safe, or out of habit. Do you know what I mean?"

"No," said Isobel.

"Why would you?" said Sally. "With someone in your life as fierce and fearless as Vincent?"

"I know," said Isobel. "Just be careful. It might not be the kind of after school special you think it is."

"I don't know what you mean by that."

"I was hoping that you might be able to tell me," said Isobel. "It's something that Vincent said. What's an after school special?"

"I don't know," said Sally. "Do you want me to check my phone?"

"No," said Isobel. "I don't want to ruin it."

"Okay," said Sally. "Do you like to go on the rides?"

"I don't remember," said Isobel. "I have trouble with my memory."

"Why don't we give them a try?"

"Sure," said Isobel.

The mall parking lot had been designed with what had been described as, "utilitarian beauty." Many people believe that parking lots are an after thought. Any leftover land is simply paved over and lines are arbitrarily painted. However, not only is there a great deal of care taken into the design of most parking lots, but the firm that designed this lot carried the Florida Pavement Association's seal of excellence. The Florida Pavement Association's rigorous vetting process means any design firm with their backing will follow not only the Florida Pavement Association's recommended practices, but will also be well within any and all State and municipal code requirements.

For example, the number of trees and other green elements placed in any given parking lot must not interfere with driver's sight lines, nor be placed in a way that may endanger property in the event of sever weather. All lighting must light the parking lot without creating shadows which may pose a threat to shoppers after dark. The relative uniformity in the design elements lent itself to a feeling of familiarity, engineering a feeling of deja vu, which put most shoppers at ease.

This was why the lighting in this parking lot mirrored that of so may others. The sterile blue green fluorescent light of every other parking lot. The lines for the cars were set at the same distances as every other parking lot. The placement of the handicapped spots were the same as every other parking lots she had ever seen. These were the same parking lots that Isobel had grown up around.

It made Isobel feel uncomfortable. She felt like there was something she was supposed to remember, but she just couldn't.

But, as Isobel came around the side of the mall to where the carnival had set up, she realized how beautiful a parking lot could be.

A colorful circus tent stood in the middle of a winding maze of games and rides, all lit with incandescent lights. The warm incandescent light shoved away the cold blue light of the fluorescents and danced across her, making her more that she had been before. Screams of joy filled her ears as people rode the Tilt-a-whirl and the Magic Express.

Why isn't the world always like this? This beautiful. This happy? Or, maybe the world is always this amazing, but we just put so much concrete over all of it, we can't feel it anymore? Or, maybe we've been blinded by the fluorescent lights? All of the beauty bleached out of the world?

"Please?" said Sally.

"Please?" said Isobel.

"Please what?" said Sally. "What did you say please about?"

"Did I say all of that out loud?"

"I don't know what all of what you're talking about," said Sally. "All I heard you say was the word please. I was just wondering what you meant when you said that?"

"I want to ride the rides, and become a part of all of this, please."

"You want to become a part of some cut rate mall carnival?" said Sally. "I think you may need to dream bigger."

Isobel thought about telling her about the Frontier, and everything it could be, but decided to wait. She didn't want to come across as needy. She was independent and she wanted her new friends to understand how she could keep them safe once they got there.

What are the odds, finding another friend in such a short amount of time?

Isobel watched as Vincent and Jimmy tentatively reached out to hold each other's hands and missed. Isobel wanted to run over and join their hands. It would be so easy to just run across the blacktop and have them link hands, but before she could, it began to lightly rain. The rain fell on the asphalt that had been baking in the sun. It was brief enough not to cause a panic. As the temperature dropped quickly, all eyes scanned the sky. There were no looming thunderstorms on the horizon.

The lone cloud passed on leaving the sweet and slightly musty smell of the rain on the dry blacktop. Isobel inhaled deeply, as she followed Vincent and Jimmy. They walked toward a line that seemed to move quickly. Before she had a chance to ask what the line was for, she was escorted to a wet seat on the Tilt-a-Whirl. Isobel smiled, the world had become too beautiful to mind the wet seats.

As the ride powered up, the seat Isobel shared with Sally swiveled back and forth, as it orbited a lit monolith. As the ride gained enough momentum, the seats whipped around. Isobel could catch glimpses of Vincent and Jimmy. Their eyes wide, exhilarated, and smiling. Isobel tried to catch their eye as they flew past, but instead continued to lock eyes with a middle aged man who didn't look happy riding with a young child she assumed was his daughter.

Every time she looked he was either staring at her, or glaring at Vincent and Jimmy. As the ride began to slow Isobel tried to get off the ride. She needed to get everyone to the next ride. It was imperative that they hurry, and probably best if they kept far away from the man with his daughter. There was something familiar in his eyes that scared her.

"Careful," said Sally, "I don't want to sound overly responsible, but I had a friend in elementary school that was decapitated on one of these because she exited the ride before she should."

"Really?" said Isobel.

"No," said Sally, as she began to giggle, "I made that up. But, the guys that run the rides will get super pissed and they might boot us from the carnival."

"Oh," said Isobel, giggling along.

The angry man grabbed his daughter and ran with her toward the exit. He looked over his shoulder at Vincent and Jimmy and scowled. Isobel was about to point him out to Sally when she grabbed her and they ran to the line for the Music Express. The angry man was ahead of them in line.

"Maybe we should skip this one and get something to eat," said Jimmy.

Isobel was about to agree when Vincent said, "Do you really think I spent this long on my outfit to have you puke all over it?"

"No," said Jimmy, "of course not. I just thought that if anyone was hungry-"

"Shh," said Vincent, as he kissed him quickly.

"Fucking disgusting," murmured the angry man.

"Maybe Jimmy is right," said Isobel. "Maybe we should go and grab something to eat."

"After the Haunted Castle," said Vincent.

"But, this is Music Express," said Isobel.

"I know," said Vincent. "Don't worry I have it all planned out."

"But," said Isobel.

"Nope," said Vincent. "This conversation is over. Relax, we're all having a wonderful time."

Isobel was having a wonderful time, when she wasn't catching a glimpse of the angry man. He seemed to be everywhere they were Not that the carnival was so large you didn't see the same faces over and over again. Isobel began trying to number them. If she could refer to them as number 6, rather than angry woman in the short shorts and flat blond hair, she might not feel quite so threatened. Behind them number 14 was whispering to number 1 (the original angry man from the Tilt-a-Whirl) while in line for the Haunted Castle. The hunted castle was an expanded semi-trailer with a small car that fit four people that disappeared into the mouth of a scary clown. At inconsistent intervals the car would shoot out of the trailer on a narrow track, as the occupants screamed and then disappear through an other opening higher up the trailer. Eventually, the car would come out where they had originally loaded everyone into it and the people would exit the ride. The outside of the trailer was decorated in the same style as her favorite shirt. She wasn't worried. There was no way that something this beautiful could possibly do her any harm.

"Goddamned, faggots," said number 1.

"Redneck asshole," said Sally.

"What the hell did you just say?" said number 1. "Watch your fucking mouth when talking around my kid."

"You started it, moron," said Sally.

Reaching the front of the line Vincent and Jimmy sat in front with Sally and Isobel behind.

The ride operator mumbled something, that Isobel assumed was close to, make sure you keep your hands inside the ride at all times, but to be honest she wasn't completely certain.

"How are you with these?" said Sally.

"I don't remember," said Isobel.

The car lurched forward, and everything was black.

"I don't get how hard it is to get someplace on time," said the child from the back seat. "I mean it is like you intentionally are trying to fuck my entire day."

"Hey," she said. "Watch your language, young man. I really don't think that is fair."

"You're right it isn't fair that I'm late to another soccer game," said the child.

"Look, it isn't that big of a deal. I called your coach, she knows we're on the way, it is going to be fine."

"It would be better if we had actually left on time," said the child.

"You know that I have trouble with my memory some times."

"Not fucking today," said the child.

"Language!"

"Why do I have to deal with you and your memories right now? Today we have the championship and you're making me late."

She didn't want to cry in front of the child. She didn't want him to know that he could make her cry. If he knew that, he would try to make her cry all the time.

She loved him, but was also fully aware at what a horrible human being she had raised. She hadn't meant to. She wanted him to be sweet. She looked in the rear view mirror. The little boy sat scowling in a soccer uniform. She recognized his face, but couldn't remember from where. She looked at her own face in the mirror and remembered where she had seen the face before. She was clearly his mother. Her smile made the tears disappear. Her eyes wandered to the other side of the back seat.

A blur.

The light changed and they were outside. Isobel blinked trying to get her eyes to adjust. Sally was screaming something at her as the car spun on the rails, racing toward a pair of doors that were slowly opening. Vincent and Jimmy were kissing again. They fell back into the darkness.

She focused on the blur, trying to get it to make sense. The harder she looked, the harder it was to see it.

"Well that sucked," said the child, as he got back into the car.

"What sucked?" she said, as she continued to make sense of the other side of the back seat.

"The game," said the child. "You remember the whole reason we fucking came out here."

"Would you mind sitting on the other side of the seat," she said.

"Why?" said the child.

"Because, I asked you nicely."

"Are you sure that's what you really want?" said the child. "I mean take a minute and really think about what it is you want, because if you really want me to sit over there I will. But, make sure you're ready for what you are about to remember. Right now, you're just fine. If you get stuck in this memory right now, you'll miss the rest of the carnival. Think of all the rides you'll miss. You've just gotten rid of one body, do you need to think about the other one?"

"Yeah," said Isobel. "But, is it my fault?"

"Why wouldn't it be your fault?" said the child. "You can remember it however you want. It won't change that you know you have blood on your hands."

She looked at her hands and said, "No, that's just hand sanitizer. Vincent wanted to use it."

"How unimaginative," said the child. "How derivative. The symbolism so fucking basic, I'm insulted that you would think you might actually have blood on your hands."

She had a stabbing feeling in her eye like an eyelash had fallen into it. She blinked trying to get it out, but her vision blurred. The world tinted pink. She looked into the rear view mirror and saw the blood beginning to dribble from the corners of her eyes. She tried to scream but her mouth was full of something salty and metallic. She opened her mouth to see what it was and blood poured down the front of her.

The child was saying something but she couldn't hear him over the screams.

"Isobel you have to get the car moving," said Sally. "I'm sorry I yelled at you , but we need to go."

Isobel looked around. She was back in her SUV, Sally sitting next to her. Her eyes were wild and panicked. Her shirt ripped with spots that looked like blood sprayed across it.

"Isobel, please," said Sally.

"Where is Vincent?" said Isobel.

Sally wiped away a tear from her cheek the said, "Do you remember why you don't like malls? Do you remember telling me all about the scary movies you watched, the one in the mall with the zombies?"

"Yes," said Isobel.

"What do you see out there?"

Isobel looked out the front windshield and saw a mass of people running toward the SUV.

"Where the hell did all of those zombies come from?" said Isobel.

"Zombies?" said Sally. "What the fuck? You want them to be zombies, fine. Just drive."

"I need to take a picture," said Isobel.

"Not now," said Sally. "Please. Isobel. Let's go."

"I'll do better than go," said Isobel, as she threw the SUV into gear and stomped on the accelerator.

"What the fuck are you doing?" screamed Sally.

"Taking care of these fucking zombies," said Isobel, as the car sped toward the crowd.

"But," said Sally, struggling to find something to say, "what if there's a cure?"

Isobel saw what she was doing, the number of people she might hurt. Granted they were zombies.

No one liked zombies.

They were like Nazis. No one sympathized with Nazis or zombies. That was why it was alright to shoot them in video games. But, if these people could be cured, then by not running them over, she would be saving them. Besides, the SUV wasn't in four wheel drive, and if too many bodies got lodged in the wheel well, she might get stuck. Then they'd be in a disabled car with a zombie horde surrounding them.

She veered left across the empty parking lot, toward the state road.

The horde followed for as long as they could. Isobel didn't mind, they had a full tank of gas and could go much faster than the zombies.

"Well done," said Sally, as she breathed a heavy sigh.

"Where do we go from here?" said Isobel. "Where do we go to make sure we're safe from the zombies?"

"Don't worry, I know just the place."

The car bumped along the state road. Isobel's head felt foggy. She looked to see if they were headed in the right direction.

"Where are we going?" said Isobel.

"I think we need to find a place to lay down," said Sally.

"It is getting late," said Isobel. "We could have gone back to the hotel. Is that where Vincent is meeting us?"

"Isobel, listen to me," said Sally.

"Isobel, listen to me," said Isobel's mother.

Isobel looked into the rear view mirror and saw that the blurry part of the seat was there. Why was the blurry part back?

"What's wrong with the back seat?" said Isobel.

"There's nothing wrong with the back seat," said Sally.

"No, look," said Isobel. "Right there, in the back seat."

Sally looked into the back seat.

"There's nothing there," said Sally.

"I know there isn't anything back there, but why is it all blurry?" said Isobel.

"Do you see part of the back seat as blurry?" said Sally.

"Do we have to do this right now?" said Isobel's mother.

Isobel turned around to see if she could find where the voice was coming from. She knew that it was probably in her head, since her mother was dead. That was something she could remember, vividly, how dead her mother was.

"You're thinking about how relived you were once I finally died, aren't you?" said Isobel's mother.

"Maybe," said Isobel.

"Maybe what?" said Sally.

"Sorry about that," said Isobel. "You may have to speak up a bit so I can hear you. I have another voice yelling at me right now. It's nothing to worry about, just my dead mother. She wants to talk to me about the blurry spot in the back seat."

"Look," said Sally. "I know that we should have stayed to help, but I just couldn't."

"Help who?" said Isobel. "Or, should it be help whom?"

"They came out of nowhere," said Sally.

Isobel tried to think what she was talking about.

They had walked off the haunted house ride.

"You seem a little shaken up," said Jimmy.

"No, I'm alright," said Isobel. "It wasn't the ride, sometimes when left alone with my own head in the dark, I can scare myself. I guess I just got a bit lo-"

A hand reached in and grabbed Jimmy. He disappeared into the crowd. Isobel turned to find Vincent as he too was swallowed up by the crowd. Isobel tried to spot them through the mass of flying arms and legs. Isobel tried to move closer, but Sally grabbed her. She wasn't sure why until she saw the blood.

Isobel slammed on the brakes.

"Did we really just leave them there?" said Isobel.

"You didn't see," said Sally. "You didn't see how badly they were hurt."

"We have to go back."

"And do what?" said Sally.

"Get out of the car," said Isobel.

"No, you don't get it," said Sally. "There was nothing we were going to be able to do back there. Let's just go somewhere and think about what we're going to do next."

"No," said Isobel. "I'm going back for Vincent and Jimmy."

"Not with how crazy that mob was," said Sally. "I'm not fucking going back." Sally scrambled out of the car. From the safety outside the car she continued, "You can do what you need to do, but I'm not fucking going back there."

Isobel looked at the young girl with sympathy. Isobel understood that Sally was frightened, but abandoning friends to angry mobs wasn't something that best friends do. Isobel knew what she was capable of, and there was no way she was going to be left alone on her voyage to the frontier.

Vincent was too important.

She spun the SUV around and headed back.

Specters tried to get her attention from the back seat, but she knew she couldn't divide her attention right now. She needed focus. If she had focused before, maybe she would have made certain that they hadn't left without Vincent. She didn't like it when other people confused her. The world was hard enough without people not telling her the truth. She needed to get back to the mall and see what happened.

The roads were getting more and more sparsely traveled the later and later it got. The analog clock that sat in the mahogany dashboard said that it was well past midnight. Of course Isobel couldn't remember if she had bothered to set the clock back this fall. The nice man at the dealership had told her that it should adjust automatically, that it had some kind of connection to an atomic clock in Denver, and you never had to set it.

She knew otherwise.

She liked it if her clocks were-

No!

Focus on the road, get to the mall, see if Vincent is still there. Make sure that his body isn't lying on the black asphalt, bleeding and bruised.

Isobel could only imagine how frightened Vincent must be. If she had been left in the parking lot she would sit down and cry and cry and cry, until she couldn't cry anymore. Or until someone came along and told her to move.

What if that had happened to Vincent?

Where could he go?

"Stop crying," said her mother. "There is nothing that can be done about that now, so just stop crying about it."

She looked into the blue eyes of the woman who was standing on the beach in front of her. She was frail, and wearing an absurd turban on her head to hide the hair loss from the chemo.

"I can't do this right now," she said. "I have to find my friend."

"You mean the faggot?" said her mother. "He's not your friend. He's using you because you keep buying him things."

"He's not a faggot," she said.

"He kissed that boy," said her mother. "That makes him a faggot, and a Arab one at that. I thought muslims couldn't do that."

"What have sex?" she said. "Of course muslims can have sex. If they couldn't have sex, how could they have kids?"

"Izzy," said her mother.

"Please don't call me that."

"You used to love it when I called you dizzy Izzy."

"No, I didn't," she said. "I never liked it, and I asked you to stop every time you did."

"You didn't!"

"Yes I did," she said.

"This isn't all about you," said her mother. "You aren't the only one here right now."

"Yes, I am," she said. "I am in the middle of driving to see if I can find Vincent. If I didn't get distracted like this maybe I wouldn't have to be looking for him."

"But, you do realize why you're here, don't you?"

"To have me feel like shit?" she said. "To have you beat me down again and again, and feel guilty because you have cancer? You're dead. You've already had the cancer. There is nothing that I can do right now to help you. The only thing that can happen right now is you hurting me, and I really don't want to be hurt right now."

"Think about it," said her mother. "I mean for fucks sake use your brain. You always were a little dense. Why be here to make you feel like shit?"

"Because, you're really good at it," she said.

"No, because you know that there is something that you need to face. You are living in denial sweetheart, and if you don't do-"

Pulling up to the Mall parking lot, Isobel saw the crowd of police vehicles surrounding the carnival. Police officers were marking off spots on the pavement, others were scanning the ground.

"Don't," said her mother.

"Don't what?" said Isobel.

"Don't stop," said her mother. "They might be looking for you."

"What if they are looking for me?" said Isobel. "I don't have anything to worry about."

"Really?"

The faceless man came at her. His face was red with anger. He spat as he screamed something about Jesus at her. She knew that this wasn't good for his blood pressure. The doctor had said that he had to avoid stress, and something else. She couldn't quite remember what the other thing was, or was it many things? If she hadn't panicked; looking at it now it would have been so much easier if she hadn't panicked. If she had just left. Even if he followed her. She had been practicing on the treadmill, and the stair climber. At the gym, she would stare at the inspirational posters on the walls. Women in perfect makeup their taught bare midriff, slightly glistening, not dripping with sweat the way that her's was. She wondered if the more abdominal muscles she showed, the less she would sweat. She felt as if she looked like she had wet her pants she sweat so much. She tried not to get annoyed with how they smiled, or how elegant they looked. She never felt that elegant when she was working out. She always felt wet and gangly. But, she knew she could run. Why didn't she?

The faceless man grabbed for her and she turned away from him, her elbow catching him in the temple. He fell, his head catching the corner of the end table with a sicking crack. The body feel to the floor with a lifeless thud.

"Really?" said her mother. "That's the way that you want to remember it?"

"That's the way it happened," said Isobel, as she pulled away from the mall.

"That was the way that you said you were going to tell the police it happened," said her mother. "But, then you saw the room and the body and realized that no one was going to believe you."

"Why should I believe you?"

"Do you remember the blood?" said her mother. "I remember the blood."

"No," she said. "I didn't."

"Then you aren't remembering what really happened."

"How the hell do you know? You're dead."

"Exactly," said her mother. "I'm just a voice in your head. If remember what happened, so do you."

"But, what if I don't want to remember, or," continued Isobel, "what if I want to remember it differently? I was the only other person in that room. What if that is the way that I decide it happened?"

"That doesn't change what really happened. No matter how badly you want it to."

Isobel didn't want to talk to her anymore. She petulantly turned on the radio, and the expensive speakers roared to life. She started to say something else, but Isobel fought to concentrate on driving along the quiet state road. In the distance, behind an abandoned restaurant, police vehicles were flashing their lights, investigating something. She briefly thought about how it looked just like the one where Vincent had helped her. She wiped away a tear, as she remembered.

"Glorp," she said under her breath. If it weren't for Vincent, her best friend, she would never have heard that sound. That was a very special bond. She tried to calm down. She would find him. He would be waiting for her at the motel. He had to be.

"Glorp," she said again, this time with a smile. She began speeding toward the motel. The Eastern horizon began to lighten, the darkness receding. As the motel came into view she saw the police cruiser in the lot.

"I always loved a sun rise," said her mother. "Don't you? There is just something about the gift that is given to us every day. That is what you keep forgetting."

She l realized she was standing on a beach again, not because of the sand, but the sawgrass scraping against itself on the sand dunes. The sounds of knives sharpening wasn't from the sawgrass, it was also her mother preparing for battle.

"You don't get it," said her mother. "How wonderful each day is, the choice on how you are going to spend you day is up to you. Now that I've developed cancer it has given me a good deal of perspective, and you need to recognize that I may have some insight, some wisdom that you can use."

"Why?" she said.

"What?" said her mother. "I'm dying of cancer, and you're going to talk to me like that?"

"Just because you're dying, it doesn't make you some kind of expert on life," she said. "And cancer doesn't magically stop you from being a horrible, manipulative person."

She began looking around frantically.

"What?" continued her mother. "What are you looking for?"

"I'm not sure," she said. "Could you please help me look for what I've lost?"

If she thought really very hard she could just make out the voices of giggling and screaming children, but no matter where she looked she couldn't find the source.

"Why the hell would I waste my time helping you look, when you treat me like this?"

"DAMNIT MOM!" she said. "Stop talking, and help me find what I've lost!"

"Fuck," said her mom. "What the fuck am I supposed to be looking for? I haven't the slightest idea what to look for!"

"Check you, Cindy Lou!" said a familiar voice.

Isobel turned and saw the most beautiful thing she had ever scene. Vincent sat, in all of his majestic glory in a beautiful red evening gown, in the seat next to her. His makeup was perfect. He looked better than he did at the carnival.

"You look fantastic," said Isobel.

"I know that, sweetheart," said Vincent. "You look like hell, and we're going to have to see what we can do about that. Where have you been?"

"Sorry," said Isobel. "Sally was scared that you were jumped at the carnival."

"Was I?" said Vincent. "Do I look like I got jumped?"

"No," said Isobel. "There isn't a mark on you."

"Oh, girl, I've been marked in all sorts of ways," said Vincent. "What do you say we blow this popsicle stand?"

"You mean leave, right?"

"Yes," said Vincent. "The frontier is calling us."

"Fucking hell, Izzy," said her mother. "I hate it when you got like this."

"Like what?" said Isobel.

"I know I'm not the only one seeing the wheels coming off this mess," said her mother. "You've always been a dumpster fire waiting to happen."

"Sweetheart, you don't have to listen to her," said Vincent. "Let's get. We've got a lot of work to do."

nine : pizza and pussy

Isobel spotted the light green letter P half a mile before she could turn into the parking lot. The SUV jumped the curb. The traction control spun the tires faster than she had intended, sending her tires squealing across the new black top. She pulled into the closest parking space, not bothering to center herself. She was so far from the entrance of the store that no one would park anywhere near where Isobel's car had landed.

Isobel jumped from the car and slammed the door behind her.

Outside the car, she breathed a heavy sigh of relief. Outside the car was quiet. A cold uninterrupted wind blew across the flat blacktop. The past week as they criss-crossed their way through central Florida, Vincent and her mother hadn't agreed on much, but for the past one hundred and thirty-seven miles they had been bickering incessantly.

"Fuck," said Isobel, as she remembered that she had left the freezer storage bag in the car. She thought briefly about reopening it, but she couldn't deal with them. She would rather deal with getting the wrong thing than having to open that car again.

Maybe I could just leave them there? What if I just found another car? Could I get to the frontier even faster without them? Without her mother. This side quest was all her idea.

Isobel imagined her home with Vincent in the frontier. Sitting on a pair of beach chairs in front of the beautiful adobe hut they built. As Isobel weaves fabric, under Vincent's direction, a small garden effortlessly grows everything they need. But, in the middle of it all obscuring her view was the bag.

An extra large resealable freezer bag.

No matter how she tried to shift her focus, she couldn't not see the plastic bag. Vincent turned to say something to her, but she couldn't make out what it was, because of the bag.

"Fuck," she said, as she walked across the parking lot toward the grocery store.

The front of the store had been decorated for the winter holidays in the most non-denominational way that a southern grocery store chain could muster. This meant that next to the towering display of Santa Claus eating a cookie shaped like a manger were a smattering of kosher items.

Isobel ignored all of it. She knew she didn't want to get lost in the sea of holiday items, not again.

She knew the grocery stores that had the big green P on them had neither a vast bulk foods section, nor an extensive collection of dried beans, but they usually had a few prepackaged bags. The ethnic grocery store she had stoped into last week had really opened her eyes in to the sheer number of possibilities and variants in both hue and size when it came to lentils. She hadn't needed any of the red lentils, she knew that they wouldn't work, but their color was so beautiful she couldn't just walk away without purchasing a bag.

"You can't keep doing that," said her mother when she got back to the car.

"Doing what?" said Isobel.

"Making unnecessary purchases," said her mother. "Every time you use that card, you're leaving a trail."

"So, you just want her to steal it?" said Vincent.

"Now you're going to be Mr. Morality?" said her mother.

"Is it difficult to be that much of a cunt?" said Vincent. "Or, does it come naturally? Sorry. What I mean is did you take classes to be this much of a miserable bitch, or does it all just roll off the tongue?"

One hundred and thirty-seven miles later, here she was. For all she knew they were still arguing. For all she cared they could kill one another.

That's a lie.

If she her mother killed Vincent, she would be heartbroken.

If, however, Vincent killed her mother...

Isobel wondered if they even noticed she had left them in the car.

She also wondered why the number one hundred and thirty-seven was important enough for her to remember it exactly.

It must be prime.

Isobel had once read somewhere that prime numbers were easier to remember than other numbers.

Why don't they just make them all prime, then they'll be easier to remember?

She was proud of this thought, as she made her way to the isle with the dried beans.

She grabbed a bag of each brand of dried green lentils she could find, both the large and the small. She even grabbed a bag of small black lentils that she thought looked like a bag of pupils if you could remove them from the rest of the eyeball. Not the pupils in the dark, when they get so wide that they let everything in, but more like the pupils when there is too much to take in. When they shrink down to little black pin pricks that stop the world from invading. They made her smile. She picked a small hole in the bag and pushed her ring finger into the bag of mini pupils. She loved the way they surrounded her finger, filing in every space around her.

Not in a scary way.

Never in a scary way.

Never in a way that made her feel trapped.

She could feel how they had protected people, how they had been the gatekeepers to other realities, limiting horrors that had been in the general vicinity.

"Excuse me," said a man at the end of the isle. "Did you find a bag with a hole in it?"

Isobel looked at him. He wore a short sleeved white shirt with a black name tag and khakis. Isobel couldn't understand how people continued to wear khakis with how obviously offensive they were.

"Fuck of you Nazi fucker," said Isobel.

She dropped the bag. As it hit the floor, the pupils turned back into lentils and they spilled across the linoleum. Isobel laughed at the joyful sound of the lentils going everywhere. Isobel hoped they would turn back into pupils once they disappeared under the shelves. She briefly wondered what they might see, before wondering if she could clarify to the man in the khakis that she was calling him a fucking Nazi, not suggesting that he had sex with Nazis.

A man at the end of the isle murmured something to someone who was just standing out of Isobel's sight-line. Isobel knew that this was her cue to leave. With six bags of lentils she walked past the checkout and out the front door.

It's gotten a lot colder. I'm going to have to think about getting a jacket.

The idea of hiding her magnificent shirt saddened her.

"Ma'am," screamed a voice behind her. "Hey! Ma'am!"

Maybe Vincent will help me find the perfect jacket?

"Hey! Stop! You need to pay for that!"

Isobel turned around to see the man in the short sleeved white shirt, black name tag and khaki pants, shivering in the cold. She reached into her pockets and pulled out a fifty dollar bill and threw it at him.

"You know earlier when I told you to, 'Fuck off Nazi fucker,' I was calling you a fucking Nazi, not suggesting that you have sex with Nazis," said Isobel, as she spun around and ran to the SUV. She felt better that she had an opportunity to explain. She didn't want to offend his sexual preferences, just his shorts.

"In the name of all that is beautiful and right with the world, tell me that man wasn't wearing khaki pants," said Vincent, as Isobel climbed into the driver's seat.

"He was," said Isobel. "I told him to fuck off and called him a Nazi."

"Check you, Frankie Foo," said Vincent. "I don't think I could actually be much prouder of you than I am right now."

"For what?" said her mother. "Being rude?"

"When it comes to khaki wearing Nazis there is no room for compassion, sweetheart," said Vincent.

"Enough!" said Isobel, more forcefully than she had actually meant to. The interior of the car was quiet. She was happy to be alone again, as she reached around to the back seat and pulled out the tall cylindrical plastic food storage container from the back seat. She opened it and blew out the little bit of dust that sat at the bottom of it. Then ripped the first bag of lentils and emptied it into the container. Isobel held it up to see if it looked right, but knew already that these lentils were too large. She opened the door to the car and emptied the container on to the asphalt. The wind picked up and blew into the car before she could close the car door. She pulled harder, slamming it shut. She opened the next bag and emptied it into the container. These were the right size, but not the right color. She opened the car door to empty these on top of the others.

"Ma'am," said the police officer, who was standing next to the SUV.

The knock at the door sounded official. There was no tentativeness in it, as of the person at the door didn't want to disturb whomever was in the house, but still wanted to get their attention. This was a knock that told the resident that they needed to get to the front door as quickly as possible, because if they didn't there would be hell to pay. As if her parents were demanding that Isobel open her bedroom door and let them in immediately.

She flung open the door.

A pair of police officers flanked a twelve year old boy who she thought looked very familiar.

"Good afternoon, ma'am," said the first officer. "Is this your son?"

"I think he might be, but I'm really not quite certain," she said.

"Well, I think we need to have a talk with his father," said the second officer.

"He's at work," she said. "What happened?"

"This is my fucking house," said the twelve year old. "This is my fucking mother, and I have had enough of this bullshit!" The boy pushed past his mother while muttering something under his breath that sounded to her like, "fucking, dumb ass bitch."

"They can be a real handful at this age," said the second officer.

"What happened?" she said.

"There was some property damage," said the first officer. "Nothing huge, but enough that paying to have it repaired is going to be a pain in the ass for your husband."

"I'm not going to pretend like we don't know what you and your family have been through," said the second officer. "If we didn't we'd be hauling that young man and his smart mouth down to lockup. For no other reason that to put the fear of God into him."

"But, everyone knows what you've all been through," said the first officer. "At this age young men have neither the emotional acumen, nor the vocabulary to really express themselves."

"Which is why boys have a mother," said the second officer. "So, that you can teach him how to deal with tragedy. I can't fathom what you and your family is going through right now, but you need to give the boy space to explore and act out, so that he can learn how none of that works. I know it is days like this where we wish they were all daughters-."

"Fuck," said the first officer. "That didn't come out the way that it was intended, sorry. I told you that line wouldn't work well."

"Yeah you did," said the second officer. "I should have listened."

"But, what did he do?" she said.

"Ma'am," continued the second officer, "right now I need you to focus in on the realities of the situation. Your son is home. He's safe. The property damage is something that can be repaired. But, if you emphasize the wrong things right now, and I really need you to hear this, if you emphasize the wrong things will you loose your son."

"I've seen it happen so many times," said the first officer. "The parents focus in on what the kid did, not what he needs to do to get better. On what he needs you to do so that he can learn the vocabulary of loss. Right now, he is learning how to deal with it, by watching the grown ups around him. It's time for you to step up and start leading by example. Do you hear what I'm saying?"

"But, what did he do?" she said.

"I hate it when they get like this," said the first officer.

"You don't have to make yourself emotionally available to help your son through this," said the second officer. "But, if you don't, everything that happens is on you."

"What a selfish, bitch," said the first officer, as they walked back across the lawn to their police cruiser.

She watched the grass bend under their heavy boots, and spring back.

"Are you alright, ma'am?" said the officer.

"Hi," said Isobel.

"Could you please step out of the car," said the police officer.

"I could," said Isobel. "But, it is getting very cold out there."

"I understand, ma'am," said the officer. "Was there an incident that occurred when you were in the grocery store?"

Isobel thought for a moment, "There was the horrible man in the khakis."

"What did he do?"

"You mean outside of wearing khakis and being a Nazi?" said Isobel. "Shouldn't that be enough?"

"Did he say anything anti-Semitic?"

"Did he need to?"

"Okay," said the officer, "outside of wearing offensive pants, did he do anything to hurt you?"

"No," said Isobel. "I left the store long before he had the chance to do that."

"Did you meant to leave the store before paying for your items?" said the officer.

"Of course not," said Isobel. "I threw more than enough money at him as I ran to my car."

"Alright," said the officer. "Would you like to press any charges?"

"No," said Isobel. "I think he probably has something wrong with him. You know what I mean? Not playing with a full deck, as people say."

"Okay," said the officer. "Do you mind if I ask what you're doing with the lentils?"

"I have to find just the right color and size."

"Dinner, or art project?"

"Somewhere between an art project and a science experiment," said Isobel. "But they have to be just right."

"Ugh, don't I know it," said the officer. "That time of year, right? I had to hit six different craft stores with my daughter to find the right kind of yarn for her science project. You would think they would wrap this shit up before Christmas break. Not like we all don't have a lot to do this time of year already, right?"

"You can say that again," said Isobel.

"Do me a favor," said the officer. "Don't dump any more lentils in this parking lot. I don't want to have to give you a ticket for littering. But, just between you and me, I wish my wife took as much interest. I mean, not just the science experiments, but also dinner. In this day and age, women that take the time to take care of their husbands are becoming rarer and rarer."

"Oh," said Isobel. "Okay."

"Good luck with all of it," said the officer. "And make sure you have a very Merry Christmas."

"And also with you," said Isobel.

Isobel closed the car door and filled the container with the third bag. She held it up. She could see the officer waving to her as he jumped into his police cruiser and drove off. Isobel focused back on the container.

Is this it? After all this time did she finally find the right lentils? The color seemed nearly perfect, as did the size.

Isobel breathed a sigh of relief as she reached under her seat for the sealed freezer bag. She took a deep breath before opening it. The smell was bad a few days ago, she was certain it could only be worse today. She fished out one of the toes and dropped it into the container, then resealed both the freezer bag and the container. She placed the remaining toes back under her seat, and looked at the container.

"That looks about perfect," said Vincent.

"But, it isn't painted," said her mother.

"What?" said Isobel.

"The one in the bulk foods section," said her mother. "That one was painted with elaborate nail art. If you want to go back and reset everything, it needs to be the same."

"What if I don't want to go back and reset everything?" said Isobel.

"Of course you do," said her mother.

"You're the one who suggested this bullshit scavenger hunt," said Isobel.

"No," said her mother. "I'm dead. This is all on you."

"So, do I need to learn how to give a pedicure?" said Isobel

"I think so," said her mother, "but if we're going to find someone to teach you how to give pedicures, could they at the very least be white?"

"What does their ethnicity have to do with how well they can give a pedicure?" said Isobel, as she pulled out of the parking space while scanning the surrounding strip malls for a nail salon.

"Nothing, but there are so many immigrants putting in salons," said her mother. "Not all of them speak the best English."

"What?" said Isobel, as she pulled the SUV into traffic.

"If you're looking for an instructor, I just think it might be best of you find one who speaks English," said her mother. "This isn't the most intuitive of tasks, you're going to have plenty of questions. And let's be honest, you've never been the quickest of studies. I remember when you took Algebra one, you were hopeless."

"You're equating getting a pedicure to Algebra?" said Isobel.

"Well, if they don't speak English it might as well be," said her mother.

"Please stop talking," said Isobel.

"Fine," said her mother. "If you don't want to talk about that, let's talk about something else, shall we? What would you like to talk about, Isobel? I know what I would like to talk about."

"Please don't."

"Why not?" said her mother. "Let's talk about what really happened! Can we do that?"

"Please," said Isobel. "Please, shut up."

"I can be quiet if you want," said her mother. "It doesn't change the fact that you fucking killed him."

"I think you're pushing too hard," said Vincent. "Even for a miserable cunt, such as yourself."

"I'm not the one who killer her husband in cold blood," said her mother. "Who thought long and hard on exactly why and how you were going to do it. If that isn't premeditation, I don't know what is. All I'm suggesting is that we start thinking about a defense. Do we want to blame it on his poor excuse of a cock? Or on his oppressive religious views? Either way, you're going to be the slut or the heathen, neither are fantastic arguments of bring to a jury."

Isobel didn't realize that she had started to cry until the first salty tear hit the corner of her mouth. She couldn't hear Vincent's protests. The world inside the car began to melt away. She thought that if she just closed her eyes, maybe she could just make it all go away. Did it matter that she was driving? All she wanted to do was make it all right again. Why did that have to be so difficult?

Isn't that what her mother always did? Even that day on the beach.

Isobel stopped. She wasn't ready.

"Look at that," said Isobel, deflecting what her mother was saying. Hoping that changing the subject might distract her from crushing what was left of her spirit. Isobel pulled into the parking lot of another generic strip mall. Flanked on both side by empty store fronts with "OPENING SOON!" signs was a nail salon.

"They don't look like they're open yet," said Vincent.

"Perfect," said Isobel. "We wouldn't want them to be open with a bunch of customers. We want to be able to ask them questions, make sure they have the time to teach us."

"I don't know where you're getting this, 'us' and 'we' thing," said her mother.

"Please don't say anything racist," said Isobel.

"Why do you assume that I would say something racist?"

"I'm going to close my eyes for a minute," said Isobel. "Wake me if anything interesting happens."

Isobel didn't know why she was so tired. It was a grey December afternoon. She felt like she had been driving for days. She tried to remember the name of the city they were in, or if they were closer to the Atlantic coast or the gulf, but the world was all a new kind of hazy since they had started the search for the perfect lentils.

And the perfect toe.

She looked at the blurry spot in the back seat, as her eyes got heavier and heavier. She was still frightened by it, but there was something comforting about knowing where something terrifying was.

There was red.

So, much red.

Then there wasn't.

She stood on top of a pile of concrete rubble. She extended her wings and flexed them. The heat from the fire that rained down on the pockmarked landscape warmed her. She looked down on the figures that cowered below her and smiled, revealing her real teeth.

The needle like rows of teeth that lined the inside of her mouth felt so much more useful than the flat molars she pretended to have. With her real teeth she could rip flesh and sever joints. With her real teeth she wouldn't have needed the bolt cutters to collect the toes.

Well, hindsight really is twenty-twenty isn't it?

She hadn't minded purchasing the first pair of bolt cutters, it was the second pair that was more annoying than it needed to be. All she wanted was a pair of bolt cutters, if everything had just gone according to plan she would have walked out with them. There wouldn't have been a need for all that red. She had told all of them that there was no reason to make any of this as difficult as they had. She wanted to say that one gender had been less difficult than the other but the smug man stocking the isle decided to prove her wrong.

"First pair not big enough?" he said with a smirk, and more innuendo than was needed.

She was annoyed that he had recognized her.

"You a metal fan, too?" he continued. "I like your shirt."

She looked down and remembered how beautiful her shirt was, and thought that maybe he wasn't all bad.

"I love metal," he said. "But, to be honest just about anything is better than the faggot ass crap you hear on the radio. Not to mention all of that rap shit."

She sighed.

"I really thought you were going to be alright," she said.

"What you like that shit music?" he said. "A metal MILF who also likes rap? You're probably lots of fun."

She walked toward the checkout.

"Look," he said, as he followed her. "I sometimes say stupid shit. How about I make it up to you?"

She stopped and looked at him.

"I could come and help you with the bolt cutters," he said. "I doubt you'll have enough strength to actually be able to get off by yourself. If you know what I mean."

She didn't.

She continued to walk to the checkout.

The man called out to someone as he ran behind her, giggling. She didn't protest when he offered to help her out to her car with the bolt cutters. She didn't protest when he climbed into the passenger seat of the SUV. Nor did she when he followed her up to her motel room. She thought about asking him his name before he shoved her against the wall and kissed her.

"Is this the help you needed?" said the breathless man.

She hit him in the side of his head with the bolt cutters. She was impressed with the velocity she had achieved with the heavy iron tool. The man slumped to his knees, dazed. Isobel raised the bolt cutters into the air and brought them down as hard as she could on his head. She smiled at the sound satisfying crack from his skull cracking. His eyes went dead and the body fell to the floor.

After removing his shoes, she tried to remove his toe using the old bolt cutter, then her new one.

She was pleased with her purchase.

Isobel opened her eyes. The world was dark, the car empty. She opened the car door and stepped out into the chilly evening. She wondered where all the tight had gone, usually the glow from the lights from the parking lots that would bleed into the night.

Isobel looked up at the nail salon that still wasn't open. She looked down at her hands. Her elegant naked fingers felt the crisp evening air, then they exploded in a flash of red. Isobel jumped and turned to see the source of the light, and saw the sign.

A sign from her childhood.

It flashed in blood red neon, then darkened. Isobel looked directly at it. She could still see the ghost image of the word, "PIZZA" dance across the world. This was the epicenter of so much joy in her young life. Birthday parties, sports banquets, and church fundraisers that wanted to insure one hundred percent participation were certain to hold them here. Isobel even remembered a promotion where you received free tokens for the video game room for every "A" on your report card. She had studied for her spelling tests all year, just for those game tokens.

Isobel danced to the front door wondering if they still had video games inside, and if the pizza tasted the way it used to?

"Are you really going in there?" said her mother.

"You don't have to come," said Isobel.

"Of course I do," said her mother. "You think I'm just going to leave you here, and wait for you out front?"

Isobel felt tiny.

Her mother smelled of stale cigarettes and sick.

"Why do you feel the need to ruin this, too?" said Isobel.

"What the hell are you talking about?" said her mother. "Why does everything have to be about you? If you need to head in there and have some crappy pizza go right ahead, but don't assume that I'm going to just hang around in a fucking parking lot waiting for you to come out."

Isobel gagged at the stench of death that was wafting from her mother.

"I'm hungry," said Isobel. "I'm going to go for pizza."

"Fine," said her mother, "but I might not be there when you get out."

"I heard you the first time," said Isobel. "If you aren't here, I'm certain we could somehow fill the void. I'll just have Vincent argue with himself, while making me feel like shit!" She flung open the door to the restaurant and walked in.

She smelled the familiar scent of stale grease, mushrooms, and beer. But, as she inhaled deeply there was another smell she couldn't quite place, it was something between bleach and coco butter.

Isobel wasn't certain if it was the veil of nostalgia giving voice to the discrete changes, or if there was something more to her trepidation. The entrance was dominated by a bear dressed like a fifties rock star holding a stringless plastic guitar. Isobel remembered the bear singing a classic rock song while gyrating its hips and moving his hands along the guitar. She didn't remember the robotic bear belting out a discordant song in German.

Isobel looked past the bear to an empty hostess area. Next to the counter were a collection of menus. Isobel reached out to pull one off the stack, and realized that the entire stack had been glued together.

Why would any one glue together a stack of menus like that? You can't open them. If you can't open them, you can't order from them.

Leaving the tower of menus, she walked along an arched hallway until she caught a glimpse of the arcade, and felt like she was ten years old again. Desperately begging for just one more token like a gambling addict needing seed money for one last score.

She followed the hallway as it twisted to a dead end. Isobel could distinctly remember a ball pit, the private birthday rooms, and the pizza room with its long benches. She always hoped she would meet someone who's parents loved them enough to rent out the private birthday room. She had heard that it had its own private animatronic band, that would sing only songs chosen by the birthday kid, and unlimited tokens and pizza.

Isobel wondered if she loved anyone enough to rent the birthday room.

Her only choice was to step into the arcade with the video game cabinets decorated with vibrant colors that would have been more at home a decade or two ago. They were lined up creating a lone path for Isobel to walk. Red light in the room made it difficult to see where the path lead her. The screens in the video game cabinets flickered to life. Instead of hearing the cacophony of hundreds of various video games, she hear moans of pleasure.

Staring back at her from the screens wasn't the sixty-four bit glory of her youth, instead it was a video of a woman pleasuring herself. Screen after screen was the same woman, repeating the same twenty-second loop. It looked like a GiF. Isobel took out her phone and took a picture of the screen. The music from the discordant German bear room began to swell the further Isobel ventured into the maze of video game cabinets.

The path turned sharply then forked. One branch had a different woman pleasuring herself, the other had a man pleasuring himself. Unsure which one to take she snapped a picture of one path, then the other.

"No photos, please," said a voice. The voice came from everywhere, but was slight and unsure of itself. "Please, treat the installation with the respect it deserves."

"I'm sorry I didn't realize that it was an installation. I just wanted some pizza."

"Really?" said the voice again. "Just the pizza?"

"Well, and play some of the video games. And get into the ball pit. Do you still have a ball pit. They never let me go it it, they always said that I was too old. But, there never seemed to be anyone else in it. I could understand having an age limit for the ball pit if you have a bunch of toddlers in it, but if it's empty why won't you just let me jump in? Sorry, am I over sharing?"

"Wow," said the voice. "Take the path with the women."

"Why?" said Isobel. "What does that lead to? The ball pit, the pizza, or the real video games?"

"They both lead to the same place," said the voice.

"Then why tell me to take one path over the other?" said Isobel.

"I thought it might make you feel more at ease," said the voice.

"Thank you?"

She walked along the corridor of women. Their moans out of sync enough it sounded more like multiple sirens going off at the same time.

A klaxon!

Isobel was proud of herself for remembering that word. She tried to remember where she had first heard it.

Must have been a word from a standardized test.

She thought back to all of the information that she had been taught for the myriad standardized tests she had taken in her lifetime. The vocabulary she had forgotten, the math problems she never used, she wondered if all of these little bits ever came back to her would she be the same person and would she like her? How much of her was made up of sixth grade English?

Isobel came to a clearing. A room full of picnic tables was surrounded on all sides by small stages with red curtains drawn in front of them. Isobel tentatively peered into the room. The curtain on the middle stage was pulled open and a collection of animals dressed as a jug band began playing an overture. The recorded melody didn't match the simplicity of the instruments the animals pretended to play. As the animals began to sing in German, Isobel ducked under one of the tables.

Under the table, the world made more sense. It was familiar. The red and white plastic table covering made fun light patterns on her arms. She looked up at what she expected to be the bottom of a wooden picnic table, but instead she saw a metal table with support beams. Isobel wondered how a table could be wood on the outside, but the metal on the inside. What were they placing on the table that was so heavy that they needed metal support on the tables? Or maybe the tables were never really made of wood to begin with? Why would they pretend that the tables were wood when they weren't? Did they paint the metal, or is it real wood attached to the metal?

"Hello?" said a voice.

"Hi," said Isobel.

"Where are you?" said the voice.

"Under here," said Isobel, as she stuck her hand out from under the table and gave a tentative wave.

"Hi," said the voice. "I heard you'd like to order a pizza. Would you like to come out and do that?"

"Why are the tables not real?" said Isobel.

"They are real," said the voice.

"No they aren't," said Isobel. "They look like wood, but they're really metal."

"I've never really given the tables that much thought," said the voice, as a smiling woman's head appeared under the table. "May I come down and you can show me what you mean?"

"Sure," said Isobel. "It is your restaurant?"

"No," said the woman as she climbed under the table. She was wearing a t-shirt that looked a size too small with a name-tag which read "Alice", a pair of short shorts, and high heeled sandals. "This place is Joel's vision."

"It's different from when I was a kid," said Isobel. "I don't remember so many naked people."

"Oh, wow," she said. "Did you come to this place as a kid? If you did, Joel is really going to want to talk to you."

"Why?" said Isobel. "Is Alice really your name?"

"Nope," she said. "My name is Mary. The Alice name tag is some kind of a joke. I would explain it if I understood it. What's your name?"

"Isobel."

"Nice to meet you, Issy," said Mary. "Would you like to order a pizza?"

"Yes please."

"Would you like to come out from under the table to order the pizza?"

"I don't think so," said Isobel.

"Well, I don't think they'll let me serve it to you under there," said Mary.

"Are there other people out there?"

"No customers, but there are plenty of folks out there. Not as many as we have over the weekends."

"What day is it today?"

"Thursday," said Mary. "I think. We usually have a pretty good sized crowd in on a Wednesday. Tuesday is ladies night. We're closed Mondays and Sundays, because we're dead and the Bible thumpers won't let us. So, I'm ninety nine percent sure that today is Thursday." Mary pulled her phone from her back pocket, and pressed a button. The screen of the phone illuminated her face. Isobel thought she was very beautiful, especially around her eyes, where she hadn't hidden her wrinkles. There was no reason such an elegant woman should hide who she really was.

"Yep," continued Mary. "I was right. Thursday. So, why don't you tell me what you want on your pizza, and what I can get you to drink? Then I can come back here and we can go topside and talk. Would you like that?"

"I think I might," said Isobel, as she took a picture of Mary with her phone.

"Why did you do that?"

"Sorry," said Isobel. "I sometimes have trouble figuring out what's real and what I'm making up in my head. You seem so nice, I'm kind of scared that you might just be in my head."

"To the best of my knowledge I'm real," said Mary.

Isobel like her. She looked down Mary's sandals and said, "That is some beautiful nail art. Did you get them done at the place next door?"

Mary's toe nails were decorated with small triangles and rainbows. The pattern reminded Isobel of an album cover for something that she wasn't allowed to listen to.

"No," said Mary. "I'm not even sure if they're officially open yet. My next door neighbor did them for me. She just did pedicures as a side job. She was working her way through school to be a vet, or a zoologist. I don't remember which."

"Oh," said Isobel.

"But there are plenty of women who would could do just as good a job," said Mary.

"I know, but if I wanted to find the woman who did that," said Isobel, "where do you think I should start?"

"Why would you need to find Kim?" said Mary. "Sounds like a hassle."

"It is," said Isobel. "But, if I want to make it all right again, it needs to be her. If she's the right one, I can get back to the way things are supposed to be. Hit the reset button. You know what I mean?"

"Nope," said Mary. "But, outside of hiding under tables you seem alright. Kim kept talking about how badly she wanted to get a job at place called Al's Gator World. She said she wanted to work somewhere where she could help make people happy. I asked her why she didn't get a job working at the big places in Orlando, instead of slumming it at a tourist trap? She said something about it being important here."

"She probably wasn't ready yet," said Isobel. " You know, to travel to the promised land you have to be ready. You have to prepare yourself in a way that you don't have to if you're just, here."

"Yep, I've never been much of a fan of here, either," said Mary. "I can look up Al's Gator World and see about getting directions."

"I love Al's Gator World," said Isobel. "I used to go there when I was a kid. The same way we used to come here. It was always a treat. Something special had to be going on. It was never something that we just did. It had to be because of a birthday party, or a field trip. I always loved field trips. They were so much fun. Until they weren't. I never did like them when they weren't very fun anymore. That was never very fun. Sometimes it was even scary."

"Okay," said Mary. "I don't think that I've ever met anyone who used to go to both places. I bet you went to Marine Land too."

"Yeah, we did," said Isobel. "At least I think we did. I have trouble with my memory. I'm not quite sure if I went there or just saw it in a movie."

"You are a hipster's dream! Joel is so going to want to talk with you, but do me a favor, don't tell him that I called him a hipster. He gets super sensitive about that."

"Okay," said Isobel.

"Do you think we could come out from under the table and talk up there? Maybe with some pizza?"

"I think that would be fantastic," said Isobel. She let herself smile. She didn't think that Mary would mind if she did.

I wonder if Vincent is going to like Mary? He won't hate her the way he hates, Mom. Maybe, as a contrast, he may love her. I'll be surprised if he meets someone he hates as much as Mom.

Isobel looked at her phone and her smile widened.

"There you are," said Isobel, showing Mary the picture she had taken of her. "You wouldn't be angry if you hadn't been there would you?"

"Surprised," she said. "But, I don't think angry. Shall we?"

"Okay," said Isobel.

Isobel let Mary lead the way.

A man with a fuzzy beard and man bun ran over to them with a pitcher of beer.

"Hello," said the man bun. "I'm Joel. Is it alright if I ask you some questions?"

"Don't crowd her," said Mary. "I just got her to come out from under the table. I don't want you scaring her back under."

"Who the hell could I scare?" said man bun, as he smiled. The smile wasn't relaxed like Mary's. His smile was forced. As if the dazzling white smile could distract from the emptiness in his eyes. Isobel made the connection immediately, his smile was the same lie as the pictures from outside the mall. She didn't like him.

"What kind of pizza do you have?" said Isobel.

"What do you mean?" said man bun. "We have regular pizza."

"Is it deep dish, New York style, pan, extra thin, traditional Italian, Detroit?" said Isobel, happy to correct the lying man.

"There's a Detroit style pizza?" said man bun.

"We have New York style pizza," said Mary. "What size do you want, and what do you want on it?"

"Just the cheese please," said Isobel.

"I think you'll definitely enjoy this beer," said man bun.

"No, thank you," said Isobel, sharper than she had meant to. "I would like orange soda please."

"Not a drinker?" said Mary.

"I don't think so," said Isobel. "Even if I was, I'm driving."

"Well, shit," said man bun, "everyone drives. What the hell do you expect people to do? Walk here? I'm not going to force you to drink, but if you want a beer, I'll just pour you one and leave it right here for you. You don't have to drink it if you don't want it."

"Don't be a pusher Joel," said Mary. "What size pizza, hon?"

"Will you have some, too?" asked Isobel.

"I would love to, sweetheart, but I'm not allowed," said Mary.

"While you're working?"

"No," said Mary. "If I want to keep working. Pizza doesn't agree with me."

"Oh," said Isobel. "I guess a medium, then."

Mary began to walk away.

"Where are you going?" said Isobel.

"Just to put the order in, then I promise I'll be right back. Okay?"

"Okay," said Isobel.

Mary walked back into the kitchen.

"So," said man bun. "What do you think."

"A lot of things," said Isobel. "Would you like my thoughts on a specific topic?"

"Yes," said man bun. "The installation. The art installation, what do you think about it? Most days we just get in young kids who pretend to not jack off to the porn on the game screens. Granted they stay for the burlesque show, but none of them grew up with this place as an institution. The irony is lost on them."

"Oh," said Isobel. "I'm sorry."

She tried to sound as dismissive as she could. She could tell that the man bun didn't want to have a long discussion about his art, but instead was fishing for someone to sympathize with the plight of the misunderstood artist. Her maternal instincts wanted to tell the young man that it was all going to be alright. However, her disgust regarding the label of "art" being slapped onto something for the sake of excusing the blatant misogyny blaring from the screens of dozens of computer screens in the maze, won the day.

"I know," said man bun. "Here you go and spend all this time and effort on putting it all together, for what? To have people just look at it like it's a tittie bar. The maze the video games cabinets create took a solid month to get right. But, this is all just your average fucking tittie bar?"

"If you didn't want people to look at it like that, then why do you have so many naked women?"

"Is it my fault that they don't grasp the irony of the situation?"

"I guess not," said Isobel. "But, what if I don't find it particularly ironic?"

"Would that be my fault?" said man bun.

"You defend your use of porn, because it is meant to be ironic?" said Isobel, proud of what a great point she was making. "But, since I don't find it ironic, is it still?"

"Yes, because I've stated that it is meant to be ironic," said man bun. "If, as the artist, I say that this is what I meant by something, then that is what I meant."

"I see that," said Isobel. "But, then whether or not you were successful would depend on if your audience saw it the same way. You can explain what you meant, but if I don't see it-"

"Well, I guess we can agree to disagree," said man bun. "The big thing I really want to ask you is regarding the authenticity of the place. I never went to one of these as a kid. My parents weren't really into places like this."

"Why did you glue the menus together?" said Isobel.

"What?" said man bun.

"And why do the tables look like wood, but are really made of metal?" said Isobel.

Mary returned to the table and placed a pitcher of orange soda in front of Isobel with a plastic glass full of ice.

"Thank you," said Isobel, as she poured herself a glass of soda.

"You're welcome," said Mary. "The pizza will take awhile. Would you like to watch some of the burlesque show?"

"Are all of the women as pretty as you?" asked Isobel.

"You're sweet," said Mary.

"Some of them are even prettier," said man bun.

"Do they have their toes painted, too?"

"Yeah," said Mary. "Kim painted all of our feet this week. We all decided to get something fun done before she left."

"I hope you don't take this the wrong way, but you do have money to pay for pizza, right?" said man bun.

"Yeah," said Isobel. "I don't have much cash on me, but I do have my husband's credit cards."

"Good," said man bun. "You just look a bit, you know, artsy. I just want to make certain that it is more of a fashion choice than circumstance."

Isobel sipped the plastic cup up soda. The sugar and orange flavor exploded across her tongue. She loved the feel of it so much she drained the cup, and poured another one.

"I'll be right back," said Isobel.

Isobel got up from the table and ran back through the maze of video game cabinets that were still blasting pornography.

Seems to me, this maze of machines is a fire hazard.

She wasn't sure why she smelled smoke, but was happy to step out into the fresh air of the parking lot.

"Check you Mary-Lou," said Vincent. He was wearing a black leather bodice, a red floor length skirt, and a long curly wig.

"I'm confused," said Isobel.

"I know you are sweetheart," said Vincent. "But, if we get in the car right now, we can escape from here right now."

"Is my mother still in the car?"

"Nope," said Vincent. "Haven't the slightest idea where she disappeared to, and to be frank, don't really care. I'm not her biggest fan."

"Neither am I," said Isobel. She opened the back of the SUV and pulled something out. "I'll be right back. If you find her, great, if you don't, it's okay."

Isobel stopped and tried to remember what else was missing.

"I miss Sally," she said. She wondered how Vincent would react. She had been so hopeful for Vincent and Jimmy.

"You don't remember?" said Vincent.

"Of course I do," said Isobel. "We left her by the place, last night."

"That wasn't last night," said Vincent. "You don't remember what happened at all do you?"

"Do you have to ruining everything?" said Isobel, as her palms started sweating. "That's not what you do. You make things better. That is what best friends do, make things better. You make me better. So, stop. Please, make me better."

"I'm sorry," said Vincent. "I'm trying. Do you want me to see if I can find your mother?"

"No," said Isobel. "Please, no. I don't want to go back to that. I'm sorry. I didn't think that with her gone that you would have to do more. I like the way that you do it better.

I've got to take care a few things then we can go remember whatever you want me to."

"Everything alright in there?" said Vincent.

"Yeah," said Isobel, as she closed the back of the SUV. "It's an art installation. Lots and lots of naked ladies."

"How's the pizza?"

"Don't know yet," said Isobel. "But, the orange soda is awesome."

Isobel headed back into the art installation with her favorite set of bolt cutters.

ten : art and artists

"Isobel," said Sally, "I need you to drive, right now!"

Isobel remembered this moment.

This was the moment when they had escaped from the mall.

When she had tried to run over the zombies and Sally didn't let her. Isobel was happy to see Sally again. She pressed the button to start the SUV and it came to life. The beeps and lights cut through the chaos to remind her that the rest of the world was only a slight depression of the accelerator away.

Isobel drove across the parking lot toward the mob. Isobel smiled. Any moment Sally would tell her to stop. Isobel looked at Sally and for the first time noticed how kind her eyes were.

Isobel jumped as the first body hit the windshield.

What is happening? Is this a dream? It has to be just a dream. Or, is it a nightmare? Is this a nightmare? Is this how I start putting things right? Do I have to make this memory right before I can make the rest of them better?

The car continued across the parking lot, rolling over a collection of bodies.

"There," said Sally, through gritted teeth, "right fucking there."

Isobel followed her finger out the blood smeared windshield and across the lot to a heavy man, who was trying to run away from the rampaging SUV. Isobel had trouble seeing through the blood, so she turned on the wipers. She was very impressed how quickly they took care of the mess.

Slamming her foot down on the accelerator caused the SUV to lurch in the direction of the fat man. They raced toward him, until he cut left. If he had been more athletic, it might have looked like a football player trying to avoid a tackle. Instead, he looked comically desperate. His expression was a mix of surprise and horror when the SUV clipped him, and he spun around and landed on the asphalt.

"Stop the car," said Sally.

Isobel did.

Sally jumped out of the car. Isobel wasn't sure what she should do next, so she sat in the car.

I wonder if Sally is like me? What does her monster look like?

Sally struggled with the body of the fat man.

"What are you trying to do?" said Isobel.

"I'm trying to get him into the car."

"Why don't you get one of the skinnier ones?"

"Because, this is his fault," said Sally. "This is this fucker's fault, and I am not going to let him get away with it. We're going to take him and make sure he never, ever forgets that this is all his fault."

"Oh," said Isobel.

"Could you help me with the body, before the rest of the mob gets here and decides we need to die, too?"

"What do you mean?" said Isobel.

"Don't worry," said Vincent. "This is just a memory. You're safe. Right now, you are months away from here."

Isobel looked at the glamorous man in the white ball gown and silver wig sitting in the seat next to her.

Of course everything is alright, Vincent is here. As long as he is right there with me, then everything was going to be okay.

The Church was near where Isobel remembered leaving Sally. It sat quietly, hidden from the highway, a collection of rotting clapboards with decades of white wash peeling from it's splintered edges. A tall cross that at one time must have been visible from the highway, now drooped to the left, its descent disrupting the earth its base had been sunk into, creating a worm filled mound of mud in the tall wild grass. Sally said it was the perfect place to do whatever she had planned.

Isobel looked at the blood stained and dented front end of the SUV.

"Wow," said Isobel. "No one's stopped me for driving a car that looks like this?"

"Nope," said Vincent. "And really, if anyone did, you could just say that you hit a deer. Or, maybe a family of deer."

"A herd of deer?" said Isobel.

"A flock?" said Vincent. "No, let's call it a murder of deer!"

"Don't make me feel bad," said Isobel.

"I don't mean to," said Vincent. "I'm just making conversation."

Isobel watched as Sally struggled with the body. The head landing on the dirt with a dull thump. The thump was nice, but it wasn't anything compared a glorp. She was certain that she wasn't going to find anything better than a glorp.

"You're right," said Vincent. "You won't find anything here as amazing as that sound."

"I know," said Isobel.

"But, don't worry, once we get to the frontier, you'll hear all sorts of things that will fill you with wonder and joy."

Isobel liked the sound of that.

Wonder and joy.

She wanted some wonder and joy.

"Can we leave now?" said Isobel.

"Sweetheart we are well on our way," said Vincent.

"Then can I just come back?"

"I wish you could, but right now you have to remember this."

"I thought you didn't want me to," said Isobel.

"I didn't," said Vincent. "But once you start something like this, you can't just stop in the middle. You have to see it through to the end. Or at least until you find me again."

"You're right here," said Isobel.

Isobel realized that she was talking to nothing.

Isobel blinked, and she was in a basement.

The basement of the old church smelled of mildew and rot. She had been surprised that the abandoned structure had a basement. Heavy metal doors had been put in place to keep out a tornado, but not the damp and decay of a Florida marsh. A palmetto bug surfed across a murky floor that at one time had been concrete, but now was slowly seceding control to the earth below. A mural along one wall showed a crowd gathered around a figure in long white robes. Most of the people surrounding the man in the white robes were dressed like rural farm hands. Isobel wondered if the figure in the white robes was supposed to be Jesus. A large chunk of plaster that should be where His head would be was missing. Isobel also wondered if Jesus was black?

Her husband liked the white Jesus.

Isobel didn't.

Maybe a black Jesus would be nicer? Or, maybe a fat Jesus? Like the fat man Sally was using duct tape to secure to the heavy chair. Isobel wondered if there was a name for the sound that duct tape makes as you pull it from the roll? She would ask Sally, but she seemed very busy.

NO! I'll paint Jesus to look like Vincent, in his most elegant evening gown! Vincent will love that! He'll understand what a special friend I can be!

"Isobel?" said Sally. "I need to go. I need to go get some things."

"Okay, I think I might need a pair of bolt cutters," said Isobel, as she eyed the fat man's sneakers. "And some paint." Isobel turned to detail her plans to restore the mural.

"Isobel," said Sally, "I need you to focus."

"Okay," said Isobel.

"Don't let him escape. Don't untie him. Don't talk to him."

"Okay," said Isobel. "But, he isn't tied he's taped."

"Then don't un-tape him."

"Okay, I'll try my best."

"I know you will," said Sally, with a forced smile that looked more like a grimace.

Sally closed the large metal doors behind her. Isobel thought about how to start restoring the mural.

Should I start with the gown? Or, would it be better if I started with the head? It would be a shame if I started with one, and make the other grossly out of proportion. Could you imagine what Vincent might think if the head dominates the mural? He'll think it looks like a caricature.

"Why the hell would you want to waste your time with that?" said the boy, as he tried to pull her away. Isobel looked around the amusement park. The horizon was dominated by roller coasters, the sounds of children screaming drowned out everything but the boy's voice.

"I thought it might be fun," she said to the boy. "And then we'll always have it to remember today."

"What in the world makes you think that I want to remember today?"

"I just thought that since we were having such a great time," she said.

"Fuck," said the boy. "I thought I would enjoy this, too. I was thinking that it might take my mind off stuff. But, you know what, every time I jump on another roller coaster, all I can do if hear her screaming. Can't you hear it?"

"Who's screaming?"

"Damnit!" said the boy. "You're doing this shit again. I wish you had an indicator light on your forehead, so I could tell when you get like this."

"Like what? Who is screaming?"

"Never mind," said the boy as he disappeared into the crowd.

Isobel moved to follow him, when she saw the blood.

It was a shallow puddle of blood in the middle of the sidewalk, a beetle of some kind squeezed through the crack in the side walk and marched through the blood. A trail of smeared blood flowed behind it. As she followed the beetle, the amusement park melted back into the basement.

Isobel wondered what the beetle was trying to show her, until it crawled over a fat sneaker. The toes in the shoe moved.

"Hi," said Isobel.

The man who was taped to the chair looked at her and tried to vocalize through a thick gag that was stuck in his mouth.

"I'm not supposed to talk with you," said Isobel. "So, there's no need for you to keep on like that. I just thought it would be impolite if I didn't say hello."

The man rocked in the chair, his eyes lit with anger as he continued to plead through the gag.

"I'm sorry I can't understand you through the gag," said Isobel. "If I take it out do you promise you won't yell lots?"

The man glared at her.

"Looks like that won't get you very far, mister," said Isobel. "There are very few things that I will not abide, one is yelling. I don't see the point in it. I think people who are trying to talk louder than other people usually don't have very much to say. The other thing I really won't waste my time with are people who wear khaki. The Nazi's wore khaki. It can be even worse if they are wearing khaki cargo shorts. My friend Vincent taught me to never trust a man in khaki cargo shorts. Do you know what I mean?"

Isobel realized who the man tied to the chair was and continued, "You remember Vincent, don't you? He was the man in the dress who you got a mob together to beat up. Do you remember him?"

He stopped screaming. His eyes met hers.

"You look like you are starting to listen, which is good," said Isobel. "I like it when people listen. Now, I'm not going to tell you that you brought all of this on yourself. That seems really mean. You know? I know someone who used to say that to me. Actually, I think it might have been more than one person. Isn't that weird, how you can combine people into the same person in your head sometimes? Anyway, as I was saying, I'm not going to say that you brought all of this on yourself, but you haven't been the nicest of persons, have you? Not that I'm being extra intolerant of your intolerance, you understand that don't you?"

He nodded.

"See, it isn't that difficult to talk to one another when we take the time to understand one another," said Isobel, as she tugged the gag out of his mouth.

"Please," said the man. "Please. Don't do this."

"Don't stumble into cliches," said Isobel. "We are making so much wonderful progress. Don't you feel like we're making progress? What is your name?"

"Tyler."

"Do people call you, Ty?"

"Sometimes," said Ty.

"Makes sense," said Isobel. "People always try to do the same with my name. I tell them over and over again, 'My name is Isobel, not Izzy!' Do they listen? So, I need you to be honest with me, do you mind if I call you, Ty?"

"No, I don't mind."

"Is it that you don't mind Ty, or do you just not want to seem difficult?" said Isobel. "You don't want to seem high maintenance, do you, Ty?"

"I guess not."

"Why?" said Isobel. "Tyler isn't an exceptionally long name. Does it really need to be shortened?"

"I've never given it much thought," said Ty.

"Wish you would," said Isobel. "I really wish you would. Here you are willing to beat the fuck out of my friend for kissing his crush, but you won't stand up to your friends for not getting your name right?"

"Jesus Christ, what do you want me to say, you crazy bitch!"

"Nope," said Isobel, as she placed the gag back over his mouth. "Are you forgetting all of the rules? These rules are in place for a reason! I'm not usually a stickler for rules. I'm not shoving you in a cold shower, because you're talking back. I'm not hitting you, because you forgot which brand is the right one to buy. Don't dismiss me as crazy. You don't get to define me. You don't get to have that power. Understand! Now, back to basics, if you're yelling you aren't listening, right?"

The man nodded his head in agreement.

"Excellent," said Isobel, as she walked around the chair. Feeling the life under her feet made her feel connected to this world. Isobel felt as if she had roots that went down to the earth's core, supporting her, helping her, making her more that what she was before.

"You have to see the world the way it is, not sit there in disgust. You need to participate, get some skin in the game, not lounging in judgement."

Isobel turned and watched as Tyler struggled in the chair. He slammed his body hard to the left, the chair tipped and his head connected with a piece of concrete with a crack.

"Really?" said Isobel's mother. "That's how you're going to remember it?"

"If that's the way that she needs to, what's wring with it?" said Vincent.

"Well, I guess if we completely ignore the fact that she's lying again, we might be able to pretend we aren't culpable," said her mother.

"We aren't," said Vincent. "She's the only one with blood on her hands."

"She needs to start facing what she is," said her mother.

"And what is that?" said Isobel. "You don't think I know what lives in side of me? I know I'm a monster."

"Then stop pretending that this just happed to you," said her mother. "You took an active roll in this, own it."

Isobel turned back to see that Tyler was still upright. He was rocking his chair back and forth. Isobel pushed him, and the chair fell over. Tyler's arms were pinned behind him as he struggled to move.

Isobel jumped on him, and looked deep into his eyes. She thought about saying something, but everything that came to mind was either a cliche or just seemed silly.

Tyler's toes came off quickly with the bolt cutters, his fingers were more problematic. With how much he struggled it was only a matter of time before she snipped something she didn't mean to. In retrospect it probably was Tyler's wrist that dulled her first set of bolt cutters. However, now she wasn't going to have to wait for Sally to get back with paint. Isobel was going to make Vincent so proud. Isobel always thought he looked best in his red ball gown.

"What the fuck happened?" said Sally, as she looked at the myriad body parts that littered one corner of the basement.

Isobel sat in the opposite corner sobbing. "I'm not exactly sure," she said. Isobel looked up at the mural and continued, "I tried my best, but I didn't have any brushes."

"It is a poor carpenter that blames his tools," said Isobel's mother. "Your artistic ambitions have always out stripped your meager talent."

"Crap, I wasn't planning on killing him, I just wanted to scare him," said Sally.

"This is why I never let your babysit your little sister," said Isobel's mother.

"Don't lie," said Isobel. "I didn't have a little sister."

"What does that have to do with anything?" said Sally.

"Sorry, sometimes my mom's voice talks a little loud in my head," said Isobel. "Sometimes it's so loud I have trouble hearing what other people are saying."

"Is she here now?" said Sally.

"Yes."

"Does she have a better idea idea what the hell happened here?" said Sally.

"I would be delighted to tell her all about what happened," said Isobel's mother.

"No," said Isobel. "She isn't the most reliable of sources."

"She tries to protect you, because she loves you?"

"No, she tries to throw me under the bus," said Isobel. "She never liked me."

"I have to love you because you're my daughter," said Isobel's mother. "But, I never liked you."

The world shifted and melted.

Isobel looked out onto crashing waves. She turned and faced the woman standing on the beach in the turban.

"Why do you keep bringing me back here?" said Isobel.

"I don't," said her mother. "It is all catching up with you. You are starting to face what kind of a monster you are, the monster that you have always been. The act surprised as it cascades all over you. Soon you'll be drowning in truth. How does that feel?"

Isobel turned to walk away from her, she realized her feet had sunk far into the wet sand of the beach.

"You can run," said her mother, "but eventually you'll sink in the sand. All it takes is a minute for you to stand still. In that slightest fraction of a minute, the flood waters finally catch up with you. Not too scary that the truth is only up to your ankles. But, as you struggle to move, you realize your feet are buried in the wet, heavy sand, and as the truth rushes in, you sink. Now it is up to your knees. Panic starts. You can't get free. The truth comes rushing in. You can't control it. Eventually the truth is going to flood in. There is no where to go. There is no high ground. You can't drive to the middle of a desert and call it the promised land."

The truth crashed over Isobel's head. She struggled for a breath as it stung her throat. Another wave slammed her down, but as she came up she was standing in front of the white clapboard church.

Isobel wondered where the smell of smoke was coming from.

"Sally?" called Isobel.

Why would she just leave me here? thought Isobel.

Isobel noticed that her SUV was parked behind her with a hose stuck into the gas tank. She pulled the hose from the tank and placed the cap back on. She sniffed to see if the smell was coming from the car. As she did, there was an explosion behind her. Not a large explosion, but enough of one to make her jump. She turned and saw the church was on fire. As she watched, the fire inhaled and there was another small explosion.

"Check you, Mary Lou," said Vincent, as he stepped out of the fire.

"I missed you," said Isobel. "Is Sally in there?"

"I think so," said Vincent.

"I painted you a picture," said Isobel. "Did you see it? It didn't turn out very good."

"I did," said Vincent. "I think it was beautiful."

"I don't know about that," said Isobel.

"I do," said Vincent. "The flames changed it into something beautiful."

"Can I see?" said Isobel.

"Not right now," said Vincent. "We have to get back."

"Do we have to go to the strip club again? I don't want to have to do that again."

"Of course not," said Vincent. "We're months away from here."

"Am I driving?"

"No, you're asleep in your car."

"Good morning!" said the man with the big, bright grin, as he tapped on Isobel's window. "You haven't been here long have you?"

Isobel looked at the man who was trying to get her attention through the window. His face was soft and round. He almost looked jovial, but his eyes and his clipboard fought against that impression. The back of the man's clipboard had a picture of a bloody man wearing a crown of thorns. He looked to be in a lot of pain. Isobel thought it looked like something right out of the horror movies that her brother had liked.

"I'm sorry, it would be a bit easier to talk to you if your rolled the window down, or came on out of the car," he said.

Isobel opened the car door to find herself parked in a lot next to an imposing glass structure. The building looked like it might have been welcomed on a futuristic city street, but here in the middle of a vast field with ample parking, it seemed out of place. The glass building towered over the distant ring of trees. The only thing taller was the cross in front of what Isobel assumed was the entrance to the building.

"You should secure that cross," said Isobel. "I was at another church where it was falling."

"Don't worry about that," said the man.

"Why?" said Isobel.

"What?" said the man.

"Why shouldn't I worry about it?" said Isobel. "Is it like an iceberg? Is there more cross below than above?"

"I haven't a clue," said the man.

"Then why shouldn't I worry about it?" said Isobel. "The way you said that, made it sound like you knew a reason why I shouldn't worry about it."

"An entire team of engineers and architects designed the Crystal House of Worship," said the man. "Every detail was examined and approved by Reverend Blackwell. This isn't some backwoods chapel fighting the rot of the swamp. That's why I don't worry about it, and neither should you."

"Okay," said Isobel. "Is it alright if I park here?"

"Right here is perfect," said the man. "I've never been a big fan of having to tell folks where to park. You know how it can be when you're organizing something like this. Unless you have a few cars visibly parked somewhere you're constantly spending the first half hour reassuring everyone that where they parked is alright. Are you here by yourself?"

"No," said Isobel. "I'm here with Vincent. I'm not sure where he is right now."

"Probably wandered off to use the facilities," said the man. "We'll get started here shortly."

"We were headed to Al's Gator World."

"Fantastic!" said the man. "We usually have so many people trying for the bigger theme parks, that we have to beg someone to go to places like Al's Gator World. Would you like some coffee and donuts while we wait?"

Isobel realized just how hungry she was. It really seemed a shame that she never got any pizza.

"Do you have any pizza?" said Isobel.

"I think right now we have coffee and donuts. There was talk of an apple fritters and bagels later. Why don't I walk you over to the table and you can see what tickles your fancy?"

"I would like that very much," said Isobel, as she closed the car door behind her and followed the man.

The blacktop gave way to a well manicured lawn, with a cobblestone path that was bordered on both sides by flowers wound its way around the cross and led to the main entrance of the glass structure.

"I love that you don't have to even think about locking your car door in this lot," said the man, bowing gently as they walked around the cross. "If it were anywhere else in town, people would think you were nuts for not locking your doors and turn on your alarm systems. I don't know who said it, but once you leave the campus it seems like everyone's motto is, 'fences make great neighbors'. Isn't that horrible?"

"The campus?"

"Yes, that's what Rev. Blackwell wants us to start referring to it. He feels if we call it a campus, then we can project the impression of learning and growth, not just one of a community built on faith. Not that we aren't. Rev. Blackwell says, "perception is reality." The more we can be seen as something more than just a church, the more tightly we become interwoven into the fabric of the community."

Next to the entrance were eight wide tables strewn with boxes of donuts and muffins, flanked by tureens of coffee. A group of women standing behind the tables busied themselves as Isobel got within ear shot. Isobel smiled at them and they averted their eyes. Isobel knew that they were all looking at her shirt. She wanted to let them know that they didn't have to be jealous, but every time they looked away she snuck another donut. She figured she could tell them once she had enough to eat.

The way they keep looking at her and looking away, made the hair stand up on the back of her neck. One woman in a pair of trendy yoga pants, whispered to another woman and giggled.

If Vincent were here he would know what to do.

"I love the shirt," said the woman in the yoga pants, as she flipped the power on one of the coffee tureens.

"You can get one at the HyperMart," said Isobel. "They had whole racks of them, no one was buying them."

The woman in the yoga pants turned to the women behind her and made a face. The women stifled giggles.

"That is some serious dedication," said the woman in the yoga pants. "I've thought about dressing the part a bit more, but I just can't bring myself to shop in 'those' places."

"I know what you mean," said another woman. "If I can't get it on-line, with next day shipping, I just don't bother."

"But, only if they have a good return policy," said the woman in the yoga pants. "If I have to do in store returns I just don't bother. Standing in line is bad enough, but having to do it with 'those' people is asinine."

"It's okay," said Isobel, trying to be helpful. "The only ones that are really scary are the clowns."

"Oh, hon," said the woman in the yoga pants, "that is vicious. You are fun!"

Isobel smiled, and tried her best to not float.

Vincent must be rubbing of on me.

Confident in her new abilities she said, "As someone who has been there, let me tell you, 'they' get very cross if you walk in through the out door, and remember, the touch screens aren't there to scare you. They're there to help you check out."

The women stared at Isobel.

Isobel ate another donut.

More people arrived, saving the women from the awkward moment. Isobel was happy that they were distracted. If they were paying attention to the new people they weren't staring at her with disapproval as she snuck another donut.

Most of the new people seemed happy. A few were excited to see one another. But, they all pretended to not be excited for the donuts and coffee. Some begrudgingly accepted the donut, then ate it greedily while no one was looking.

Isobel grabbed an entire box of donuts, and said to the woman in the yoga pants, "Making sure the people in the back get some." Isobel smiled as she walked toward the back of the crowd, making a big show of offering a donut to a couple of people before she had another one herself.

She turned to find she was standing by the man who had tapped on her window. Isobel smiled at him and she offered him a donut.

He glared at her.

She ate another donut.

He began waving his arms at the crowd to get their attention.

"Hello," he said. "If I could get everyone's attention! Please I know you are all very excited, but if you could all just quiet down for a second, I have a few announcements to make before we get the pastor out here to give us his blessing."

Isobel scanned the crowd for Vincent. She knew he wasn't far, he wasn't ever far away. But, she wondered why she couldn't find him.

Don't panic. He hasn't left. Mom didn't come out of nowhere and steal him away. She couldn't do that. Could she? Would she? She knows how important Vincent is to me.

"I am so happy to see so many people here," continued the man. "I am always surprised at how blessed we are to have so much support. That being said, make sure everyone has had enough before you head back for seconds. I know that these donuts are delicious, and thank you to Meg for bringing the coffee. But, she didn't do it to make sure you had breakfast, this is just a snack before we load up on the busses and cars to get to the attractions. It is thanks to you that our, 'Monetization of Joy' protest will be a success!"

Isobel tried to not panic. She felt her hands begin to shake and sweat.

"I know that many of you are very excited about this," he continued. "I also know that there are some of you who are here to get a free pass to some of the larger theme parks in Orlando. I completely understand this. And I encourage you to enjoy yourself, however I need you to make certain that you keep in mind what our mission. To those of you who have already requested some of the smaller attractions in the area, I applaud your dedication to our cause. Ladies and gentlemen, it is with a full heart and united with you in faith that I introduce, Reverend Blackwell!"

Isobel was surprised by his tone. He sounded more like he was introducing a band than a pastor. The crowd's reaction was full of screams and tears of adulation.

A man who Isobel assumed was the Revered Blackwell walked out, and to Isobel's joy Vincent followed him. She began smiling and applauding as well. Vincent took a quiet bow and winked at Isobel. The relief washed over her, and she felt light headed. She wondered if it was the adrenaline leaving her, or if it was coming down off the sugar rush that was making the world iris to black.

"Lady, you need to move your cart," said the kid in the green apron.

"What?" said Isobel. She looked around and saw that she was standing in the middle of the isle of a grocery store.

"The isle," said the kid. "No one can get past and there are other customers that want to shop the bulk foods isle."

A row of clear plastic containers filled with nuts, grains, and assorted legumes called to her, demanding her attention. She wanted to yell that none of this was her fault. That if anyone, or anything was to blame it would be something down this isle. She glared at the plastic, as if she could will it into admitting to everyone that this wasn't her fault.

Really, how hard could it be to admit that I'm not the one at fault here?

"Ma'am," said the kid again.

"Would it really be that hard?" said Isobel, as she turned on the kid in the green apron. "To just admit, for once, that this wasn't my fault. That I'm not the loopy one here! God, I hate saying loopy. I feel like I sound like I'm seven. I'm a fourt year old woman, I should be able to say what ever the hell I want. But, my therapist says I shouldn't say, 'crazy.' She says it's hurtful. I think it's probably only hurtful if you are crazy. You know what I mean? Do you find it hurtful?"

"I just stock the isle, ma'am," said the kid. "I'm not qualified to discuss mental health with you. This is only my first week. They haven't even taught me to use the registers yet. Stocking this isle is my goal for the day."

"Goal for the day?"

"Yeah, we have to make a list of the items to complete for the day," said the kid. "Based on that we're graded. The managers understand that you're not going to get a hundred percent of your goals done every day. But, if you keep falling below fifty percent, then they start thinking about putting you on THE list. And I don't want to be on THE list my first week."

"THE list?"

"Yeah," said the kid.

"I'm trying to understand and you're talking to me about lists?"

"Well, it's important to me," said the kid. "Now are you on the list?"

"What?" said Isobel.

"I'll check again," said the kid in a voice that wasn't his, "but, her name isn't on the list."

Isobel opened her eyes.

She blinked, trying to wash the fog from her eyes. As the world came into focus she saw a flying baby in a loin cloth.

That's new, I don't remember ever hallucinating about flying babies. At least. never about happy flying babies. There was the one time I had that dream about the vampire babies, but these don't look like that.

Next to the babies was a man in a three piece suit. Isobel focused in on the man in the suit. His face looked kind. His eyes soft and inviting. He was reaching out a hand toward an old man in a beard who was also in a suit. The more that Isobel looked at it the more she realized it looked like the Sistine Chapel, but cheap. As if someone wanted to recreate the Sistine Chapel, but didn't want to pay for any trained artists.

"Well, if she isn't on either list, does it really matter?" said the voice Isobel recognized as the man who had tapped on her window. "She might be new, and if she were some kind of infiltrator why would she say she wanted to go to Al's Gator World? Nobody wants to go to that shit hole."

"Please watch you language," said a new voice.

"Fine, are you going to go to Al's Gator World in her place?" said the man.

"She isn't on the list," said the new voice.

"She isn't on the enemy list either," said the man. "So why don't you just relax and let's see how she is once she wakes up."

Isobel realized she must be lying on a floor looking up at a ceiling. She pulled her phone from her pocket and took a picture of the mural.

Isobel sat up. She was in a cavernous room decorated with red velvet furniture.

Red velvet seems a little heavy for Florida. How do you get the sweat smell out of it?

"Hi there," said the Reverend Blackwell. "You took quite a tumble there, are you feeling alright?"

The Reverend was standing over her with the man with the clipboard.

"Yes," said Isobel. "I was about to have a panic attack, but I didn't. When I didn't, all of the adrenaline left me. Must have happened as I came down off that sugar rush, never could refuse a donut, and I guess I got a little lightheaded. It was the first meal I've had in awhile."

"Are you having a hard time of it?" said Rev. Blackwell. "I mean, are you homeless or hungry? Is the reason you didn't have dinner because you can't afford it?"

"No, it was because I didn't realize it was a strip club," said Isobel. "It looked just like a pizza place from my childhood, but it wasn't."

"Max, you remember when I told you how that place was going to be nothing but a blight on the community as a whole," said Rev. Blackwell.

"I do," said the man who Isobel now assumed was Max.

"Why did you paint your ceiling?" said Isobel. "It doesn't make much sense to have this great glass building if you're going to paint the ceilings."

"Why, don't you like it?" said Rev. Blackwell.

"No," said Isobel. "I saw a mural on a wall of church in a field that I did like. That one was pretty. I had a lot of trouble making it better it was so beautiful."

"Are you an artist or a restorer?" said Max.

Isobel loved the idea of being called an artist. The possibility that anything she did could be described as art filled her with so much joy she laughed.

"I'm not a restorer," said Isobel. "I'm want to be good at making things better, Vincent it really good at that. But, I think I'm an artist. I loved standing close to the paintings at the museums. I don't remember if it was because I was studying the brush strokes, of if it was just really fun when grown ups get nervous when you stand close too stuff like that. You know what I mean?"

"I'm not sure-" said Max.

"I like," continued Isobel, "to make something new, something beautiful. Even if you might not think it is beautiful. If you want, I could make your ceiling beautiful. I wouldn't be as hard as the church in the field. They didn't have people in suits. I don't like the people in the suits. And I don't like how everyone looks the same."

"The artist based all of the faces on the founding members of our congregation," said Rev. Blackwell. "If you look hard you'll see that I'm up there, along with Max, and some of our other donors. However, I feel that the holy spirit has brought us together. Max and I had just been discussing our desire to add in some new figures to the mural."

"And maybe take a few out," said Max.

"I am happy to meet a muralist," said Rev. Blackwell. "Hopefully, this will be a fortuitous introduction."

"I'm sorry, I shouldn't be prejudiced against the Jesus in a suit," said Isobel. "But, I've never seen a Jesus in a suit before. My husband liked the white Jesus. I don't much care for him, but I think that was more because of my husband than the Jesus, do you know what I mean?"

"Sure?" said Max.

Isobel wondered why he drew the word out and shot a look at the Reverend.

"Is your husband with you today?" said the Rev. Blackwell.

"His name is Vincent," said Max. "Is that right? You said you were looking for someone named Vincent."

"Vincent isn't my husband," said Isobel. "Vincent is my best friend, but I don't know where he's disappeared to."

"You didn't see him around the coffee?" said Max.

"No, Vincent snuck on stage while Reverend Blackwell was giving his speech," said Isobel. "I was so relived to see him. He looked beautiful in that evening gown!"

"You saw a fag in an evening gown on stage with us?" said Max.

"I'm not completely certain of Vincent's sexuality," said Isobel. "But, I do know he's Arab."

"Fucking artists keep the weirdest company," said Max.

"There is nothing weird about Vincent," said Isobel. "He is magnificent and my best friend."

"Okay," said Rev. Blackwell. "I think we're done here."

"Oh," said Isobel. "Sorry, if you don't want to talk about your celling anymore. I just thought it was kind of weird. I mean you have all of these naked kids and babies, but everyone else is in a suit. Not that it wouldn't be weird if the men were naked and the kids were wearing suits. I never like it when people dress babies like grown ups. Are there any women up there? I wouldn't want to assume that there weren't if there actually were."

Max and the Rev. Blackwell stared at here.

"Anyway," she continued, "I'll just find Vincent and we can be on our way to Al's Gator World. I'm excited to show it to him. I loved it as a kid. We also need to find a pedicurist. I'm not sure if she's Asian or not. My mother would just assume that we should look for the first Asian woman we can find working there, and she'll be the one to paint the toes. But, not until I show Vincent how fantastic Al's Gator World is."

"So, you just came here for the free tickets?" said Max.

"No," said Isobel. "I would have been happy to get my own tickets. I think Vincent and I pulled into the parking lot to take a nap. You're the one who said I was here for the tickets. And why would you want to stop people for being happy?"

"We aren't trying to stop people from being happy," said Max. "We just want them to be happy from the right things. But, now I think it is time for you to leave."

"Drive safe," said Rev. Blackwell.

"But, you haven't helped me find Vincent," said Isobel.

"Don't worry," said Max. "He's not here."

"Are you sure," said Isobel. "This seems like a really big place."

"Oh, yes," said Max. "We're positive."

"I guess I should just go then," said Isobel.

"I think that would be for the best," said Max.

"Thank you for the donuts," said Isobel.

"Oh, you're very welcome," said Max. "Sorry this didn't work out."

Isobel began backing toward where she assumed a hallway would be.

"That's alright," said Rev. Blackwell. "We'll have some one see you out."

"That won't be necessary," said Isobel. "I'm certain I can find it."

"No," said the Rev. Blackwell, as a sharpness entered his tone. "We'll have someone show you out. You were passed out when they brought you in and I'm certain you don't know the way."

"VINCENT!" screamed Isobel, as she ran from the men.

"Where do you find them?" said Rev. Blackwell.

"Let's just help her find her friend," said Max.

"No, she leaves now," said Rev. Blackwell.

A pair of security guards ran into the room and grabbed Isobel. Their hands were rough and calloused. The Reverend Blackwell's moth broke into a flawless smile, as they walked her toward the exit. Their movement was so sudden and forceful that she didn't have time to transform.

She blinked twice and she was outside.

Gilded doors she hadn't noticed before, closed in her face. She looked behind her to see her SUV and Vincent standing next to it in a light blue pant suit.

"Check you, Mary Lou!" said Vincent, as Isobel got closer to the car. "Making all kinds of friends when I'm away."

"Vincent, don't tell my mom, but I think I'm an artist now," said Isobel.

"Is that what you want to be?" said Vincent.

"I think it is," said Isobel.

"Then I think it is fantastic," said Vincent. "Who were those people?"

"They were going to give us free tickets for Al's Gator World," said Isobel. "It had something to do with them wanting people to be happy in the right way."

"Why do they think we would need a hand out?" said Vincent. "And what is the right way to be happy."

"It was because of how many damned donuts she ate," said Isobel's mother. "And I think anal sex would be high on their list of things they don't approve of. For that matter, most anything to deal with fagots would be on their no-no list."

"Fuck!" said Isobel, as she climbed into the SUV. "Where the hell have you been hiding?"

"Don't worry about that," said her mother. "You should drive before you make the nice people angry and they call the police."

"We haven't done anything wrong, except eat too many donuts."

"There's a bag of toes under your seat that may dispute that," said her mother. "Now, drive."

eleven : eat me, drink me

Isobel wondered if the empty field was farmland, home for a future subdivision, or would be a new strip mall. Isobel tried to remember if she had actually once been excited about the opening of a new mall, or if she had simply been playing to her established stereotype.

"If the good Lord didn't want us to go shopping," said the faceless figure that she still assumed was her husband, "he wouldn't have given us such an abundance."

"So Jesus wants me to go shopping?" said Isobel. She didn't mean to sound so skeptical. She regretted her tone as soon as she had said it.

"Fuck, Mom!" said the young boy who was sitting next to her. "Why do you have to fucking ruin this? It is a fucking mall. He wants you to go shopping. Fucking go."

"I really don't like you using that word," said Isobel.

"Which one?" said the child. "Fuck? Well, fuck, if you don't fucking like it then what the fuck am I going to do?"

"I think that's enough," said Isobel.

"What is?" said the child. "Me saying fuck? You're not going to remember it in five minutes anyway. Hell, you're not going to fucking remember me in five minutes you crazy bitch!"

"Stop it!" screamed Isobel.

"You don't get to tell me what to do," said the faceless man. "Don't doubt what I tell you about the Lord. That is not, and will never be your place."

"Wait," said Isobel. "What's happening? I don't understand what's happening right now. Where is the child?"

"Which one?" said the faceless man.

"There was only the boy," said Isobel.

"You dumb, bitch," said the boy. "You don't remember do you?"

"I'm sorry, I have trouble with my memory," said Isobel.

"No," said the boy, as he changed into the faceless man. "You don't get to do this. Not again."

"Why?" said Isobel. "What am I doing, and what don't you like about it?"

"The abundance we have has come because of His love and grace," said the faceless man. "You must accept that this is what our life is, and stop railing against it. The same grace that has been bestowed upon us for this is the same that has-" The faceless man trailed off.

"Has what?" said Isobel. "Made me?"

"Don't make me say it Isobel," said the faceless man. "I hate the way you are, but this is the way that God made you. It is my duty to make you better."

Isobel looked herself over.

Why does everyone think there is something wrong with me? I'm not broken.

"Vincent doesn't want to fix me," said Isobel, as she turned on the faceless man. "Why do you?"

"He's not real."

Isobel looked out the cracked windscreen of the dented SUV and saw another billboard announcing the imminent arrival of Al's Gator World.

"Check you, Cindy Lou," said Vincent, from the passenger seat.

Isobel fumbled with her phone, and the SUV swerved and slid on the damp early morning pavement.

"Do you really want to know?" said Vincent.

"I guess I should," said Isobel.

"That isn't want I asked," said Vincent. "What I want to know is if you really want to know."

Isobel put her phone back in her pocket.

"Would you go away?" said Isobel.

"I'm not exactly sure," said Vincent. "But, I'm here now. And I look fabulous, don't you think?"

Isobel looked at the pink poodle skirt, fuzzy matching sweater, and beehive Vincent was wearing and giggled.

"What's wrong?" said Vincent, suddenly looking more vulnerable than Isobel had ever seen him. She liked the idea that now she could be the strong one,

the artist who could make everything alright.

"There's nothing wrong," said Isobel's mother appearing in the back seat across from the blind spot. "She's just happy and giggly. I think you look like a moron, faggot."

"Hey," said Isobel, as she fumbled her phone out of her pocket. The SUV swerved off the asphalt and kicked up pebbles on the shoulder. She steadied the car then, took a series of pictures of the back seat. "What do you think will happen now? Once I find out she's just in my head? Do you think she'll finally just disappear? Or, will we have to continue to endure her ignorance regarding your choices?"

"Are you really going to pick that over me?" said her mother. "Your own flesh and blood over-"

"Please don't embarrass me further by saying something even more ignorant," said Isobel, fulling expecting her mother to say something in a huff before stomping off. But, the back seat was quiet. Isobel stole a peek in the rear view mirror. Her mother was gone, but the fuzzy spot on the back seat was still there.

I should probably figure out what that fuzzy spot is.

"Come see GOLIATH! World's oldest and largest Gator themed WILDLIFE SANCTUARY!" it read.

Isobel could visibly see where they had added the words, "wildlife sanctuary." She tried to remember what had been there before. What had they called it to get people to stop? Zoo? Attraction? Park?

"Tourist trap?" suggested Vincent.

"No," said Isobel. "That would just be silly. Who would stop for something that was called a tourist trap."

"Thank you for standing up for me," said Vincent.

"Nope," said Isobel. "You don't thank me for doing the right thing. Keeping you safe and making sure people respect you and your choices are the bare minimum that I have to preform from one human being to another."

Isobel liked who she was becoming.

A billboard with an arrow pointing down a dirt path directed Isobel toward the parking lot. As the SUV bumped along the dirt rivets wide flat fields clung to a blanket of fog that would burn off quickly. The sun refracted through the fog, dancing across the world making it brighter, but hazier. Everything a few meters away disappeared into an elusive undefined nothing, as if the world weren't done. As she inched closer the world was being taken from her memories and stitched together just out of sight. The finishing touches put on it just in time for it to be revealed.

The idea of beautiful formless creatures making the world in the black nothing that existed only seconds before Isobel had an opportunity to see it excited Isobel. She sped up the car and began scanning the horizon more erratically, hoping to catch a glimpse of the absence of everything. A formless world full of possibility. Not one where everything was dictated by the meter or two that proceeded it. Yes, with all probability the next meter of road would look a lot like the previous meter of road; the same dirt rivets cutting across a similar field leading to a vaguely remembered dirt lot and alligator park. But, if the world just on the other side of the fog is being created right now, then couldn't the world could be anything? Pink grass with sugar rock pebble roads that get tacky in the summer sun. The world sticking to the bottom of your shoes until you have to stop and lick the sugar off. Or, fire raining from the sky with majestic flying beasts beating their wings and circling just out of reach, as you slowly sink into oblivion in endless pools of molten sugar. Desperately reaching for help that you know will never come.

If this was the world she was falling toward, she could finally be whatever she needed to be, not what the world expected her to be. She could be the monster in side of her any time she wanted. She could have extra arms instead of breasts, she wasn't planning on having more children, an extra pair of arms would be much more useful.

Turing onto the dirt lot, the fog began to melt away. Isobel leapt from her car and ran through the empty lot letting the possibility of the world fill her.

"Ma'am," said a young man in a green apron.

Isobel fought back her scream. She didn't want to fall backwards into the grocery store. Not like this, not without the toe. But, as the panic washed over her she noticed the young man's background wasn't filled with isles of products, but instead a concrete Alligator mouth.

"Good morning, ma'am," said the young man in the green apron. "I hope I didn't startle you. The shuttle parking for the other Orlando attractions has been moved up the state road just a bit."

"Oh," said Isobel. "I'm here for Al's Gator World."

"Really?" said the kid in the apron. "Folks don't usually come here until after they've done the other stuff in Orlando, or if the other stuff is super crowded."

"No," said Isobel. "I'm here for you."

"Oh, well I hope you're not disappointed," said the kid.

"Why, are you closed?" said Isobel.

"No," said the kid. "We are totally open, but just so you are aware, it does kind of suck."

"How could you possibly say that?" said Isobel. "You work at one of the most amazing theme parks in Florida."

"Spoken as someone who hasn't see what the rest of the greater Orlando/Kissamee area has to offer."

"I have," said Isobel. "I went with my family, and I'll be honest, they bored me. Sure they have plenty of long lines and technological marvels, but there isn't anything very Florida about any of them. If it wasn't for the humidity how the hell are you supposed to know that you're actually in Florida? No give me a place like Al's Gator World, full of lost tourists and a gift store with vaguely racist ashtrays and dead animals in formaldehyde! That's the place for me."

"Oh," said the kid. "Just so you know we've gotten rid of the racist ashtrays. Some guys from the NAACP came through last week with a film crew, and made us."

"That's okay," said Isobel. "They made me kind of uncomfortable, and I'm certain they would make Vincent feel very uncomfortable."

"Who's Vincent, your son?"

Isobel threw her head back in a wild guffaw, "No, Vincent is my best friend. He's probably just wandered off. He'll be back shortly. But, when he does, please don't make a big deal out of the way he's dressed. Unless, you want to compliment him. If you want to do that, feel free. Lately, he has been wearing a lot of ball gowns, so if you want to say he looks nice that will be fine. But, don't be too complimentary. He just got out a relationship. Pretty violently. I don't think he's really ready for a relationship with someone new. He's fragile right now, and that's why he has me to help protect him."

"What the fuck is wrong with you?" said the kid. "I'm not gay."

"I'm not saying you are," said Isobel. "I'm saying my friend is fragile right now. If you are going to help me today you are going to have to understand that. We are going to have to protect Vincent. Do you get that?"

A line of cars entered the lot.

"You may purchase your tickets at the counter in the gift shop, located inside the alligator's mouth," said the kid. "I hope you enjoy your visit."

Isobel felt the kid must be under a lot of pressure, but still he shouldn't be so surprised that people are coming where he works.

"Does it seem strange that he's about as surprised that we're here as I am?" said Vincent.

"He must be new," said Isobel. "Don't worry, nothing is going to happen to you."

"I know," said Vincent. "Just abject boredom."

"I promise you," said Isobel, "if you give it a chance, you'll love it."

"Isobel?" said a woman's voice.

Isobel turned to see a woman getting out of an SUV that was similar to Isobel's, but without the dents or the blood. She had a pleasant round face she wore as a mask to hide her disappointment and judgement.

"Umm," said Isobel, searching for the woman's name, but unable to remember.

"What the hell happened to you and George?" continued the woman, as she crossed the dirt lot toward Isobel. As she dug her small pink shoes into the dirt to gain tractions she kicked up small plumes of dust. Isobel thought she looked like a charging peach colored bull.

"I'm not sure if I know you," said Isobel, as she pulled her cell phone from her pocket and tried to discreetly take a picture of the woman who was soon going to be crowding her personal space.

"Of course you do," said the woman. "Or should I say you will. I'm Marjorie, I lived next door to you and George for years, before the accident. Now, I didn't mean to listen to a lot of the gossip, but I heard that you went off the deep end and left. But, to me that just didn't sound like you. You wouldn't just up and leave the only kid you had left now would you."

"Marge?" said a heavy man who was trying to catch his breath as he walked up behind her. "What the hell are you doing? Why don't you leave that nice woman alone."

"Damnit, Jim," said Marjorie. "Can't you see who it is?"

"Nope," said Jim, as she finally reached them. Isobel thought it strange that he was sweating as heavily as he was.

"It's Isobel," said Marjorie. "Where is George? And Sam? Where is Sam? He was always such a nice boy."

"Are you talking about that mouthy neighbor kid," said Jim. "He was a fucking asshole."

"Damnit, Jim!" said Marjorie. "You're talking to his mother."

"No, I'm not," said Jim. "This isn't Isobel. Isobel was one of those blond busy bodies constantly buzzing around the HOA and the PTA meeting trying to get us to participate some bit of bullshit or another."

"Who the hell do you think this is then?" said Marjorie.

Isobel looked deep in his eyes and tried to will him to say that she was.

A monster?

An artist?

She didn't care, she just wanted to finally see her.

"Fuck if I know," said Jim. "Hurry up, or we'll miss the tram."

Marjorie, looked at Isobel. Marjorie's mask faltered.

"I think I may want to see this place first," said Marjorie.

"Why the hell would you want to do that?" said Jim.

"You remember how Isobel had issues with her memory," said Marjorie. "What if she just doesn't remember who we are, or where she left her husband, or why she abandoned her kid?"

"First," said Jim. "I don't think this is her."

"It is," said Marjorie.

"Fine, if it is Isobel, then she was smart to get the hell away from that pencil dick whack job of a husband and asshole of a kid, and it isn't any of our fucking business."

"But-" said Marjorie.

"But what?" said Jim. "Your grand kids are meeting us at the park. Do you want to waste your time here with a woman who has no desire to remember you or the life she left behind, or do you want to get your fat ass on the tram so we can make it to the monorail?"

Marjorie's face turned red and she said, "Before I go, I just need to say I have no idea how you could ever-"

"Alright," said Jim, as he spun her around and began walking her toward the waiting tram. "Good luck," he screamed over his shoulder back at Isobel. "I hope it all works out."

Isobel walked toward the massive concrete alligator head, scanning the parking lot to see if she could see Vincent anywhere. She pulled out her phone and looked at the pictures of Marjorie and Jim. Just outside of the world she could hear a voice that sounded like her mother. Isobel wondered if she could escape it by ducking into the cedar lined gift shop.

Standing there a pit of black opened up inside her, but before it could swallow her she knew she needed to see what would happen if she looked at the pictures she had taken of the back seat. Then she would know if Vincent could stay if she wanted him to.

She looked at the first picture and saw that her mother wasn't in the back seat. The black began to recede, until she continued to scroll through the burst of pictures from the back seat.

How?

How could she have forgotten?

Why did she forget?

Because. She needed to.

The parking lot melted into the beach.

"You need to understand that I'm dying," said her mother, standing on the beach. The wind shifted causing the sawgrass to scrape against itself. To Isobel it sounded like sharpening knives, but she also knew what was going to happen.

The sky darkened.

"Mom," said Isobel. "I need to go and check on Jess."

"You can't go running off every time I need to talk to you about my wishes," said her mother. The increasing wind caught her turban, and it few into the knives on the dunes. Her balding head had only a few patches of white hair left. Her face both gaunt from the chemotherapy and puffy from the steroids twisted in anger and embarrassment.

"It isn't that," said Isobel. "Sam is in this stage of being an asshole and doesn't bother to watch her, and you know how she gets when she's around water. Let me just get in sight of them, then you can continue to tell me how you want me to mourn you."

"George can keep an eye on them," said her mother. "How can you be this flip about everything when I'm dying."

"I'm not being flip, I'm just trying to keep an eye on my kids. The water is getting rough."

"Of course," said her mother. "A storm is coming."

"Do you see her?" said Isobel, trying to control her panic. "I don't see her, do you?"

"She's fine," said her mother. "You need to relax."

"No," said Isobel. "You don't get to fucking do that. You don't get to make me a neurotic mess, then tell me to relax."

"Blaming it all on everyone else again?" said her mother. "How is that working out with you?"

Isobel heard the whistles.

Then she ran.

Her legs trying to gain purchase on the shifting sands.

Plumes of sand kicked up behind her.

Her legs burned as she tried to will herself to be faster.

You'll never be fast enough. No matter how hard you try, you will never be fast enough to out run this. You will never be fast enough, or go far enough to ever get away.

The body.

So, tiny.

Her everything was ripped in half. She tried to hold the child's body to her raw tattered soul, but her arms passed through her.

"Where were you?" said the faceless man, as he turned red. "I always hate it when you go to the beach, because something always happens!"

"Mom wanted to have a talk with me," said Isobel. "The sawgrass sounded like knives. She was just making them sharper with every word. I tried to break away, but she wouldn't stop talking."

His hand darted through her line of sight connecting with her cheek.

"You don't get to do that," said the faceless man. "You don't get to do that. You don't get to blame the death of our daughter on your mother. You don't get to do that. That poor woman died of cancer."

Isobel wondered why he didn't understand what had happened.

"You need to talk to someone," said the faceless man. "I don't know why God made you the way that he did, but something is just not working right when it comes to you. Do you get that."

Isobel wanted him to stop talking, all she wanted to do was hold her daughter. She reached down to grab the body, and passed through it again.

"Izzy," said the faceless man. "You need to stop. Stand up."

"How can you be this relaxed about this?" said Isobel.

"Is she having one of her fucking episodes again?" said the young boy standing next to the faceless man. "I fucking hate it when you act like this."

"Watch your language!" said Isobel.

"Watch your crazy!" said the boy. "You get to fly completely off the handle, but I drop an f-bomb and everyone looses their fucking mind."

"It just happened," said Isobel. "Let me mourn this!"

"It's been years," said the boy. "This didn't just happen. You keep slipping back to that moment and getting stuck."

"But, I can still hear the sawgrass," said Isobel.

"It always starts with that," said the faceless man. "Let me ask you this, can you make out my features?"

"Why would you ask that?" said Isobel.

"You are spiraling out of control," said the faceless man. "Your therapist said this might happen. If you face the pain, if you accept this as your subjective reality, then you can get better. If you keep denying the real world then what hope is there for you? What hope is there for us?"

"I think that the best course of action would be for us to schedule a longer session next time," said her therapist. She sat behind her pressboard desk on the beach, and flipped through her calendar. Each page scraped against the spiral metal clasps that held the paper inside the note book. Isobel thought it sounded like the sawgrass.

"Why don't you help me?" said Isobel She looked from the blank face of her husband to the annoyed child to her therapist trying to find any compassion she could use to help her hold the body and heal? They all looked past her, just over her shoulder to where she would be, where they thought she should be, not accepting where she was.

"Please," continued Isobel, as the continued to not see her.

"We've got a plethora of options here," said her Therapist, as her desk moved past Isobel and the body.

The faceless man followed the woman at the desk, and said, "Are any of them, and I want to sound as compassionate as possible, minimally disruptive? We've already been through a lot with her, and having to do more, eat me, drink me, sounds exhausting."

Isobel pawed at the sand hoping that this time she might not pass through the body. Tears streamed down her cheeks and landed on the child, so why couldn't her hands? Why couldn't she make herself whole again?

"I know your pain," said her Therapist. "She's broken, and you want to mend her. Eat me, drink me."

"I'm not broken," said Isobel. "I'm different now."

"We've prayed on it, daily," said the faceless man. "But, she doesn't eat me, drink me, hard enough. If she had more faith, or really wanted to get better, she would. That's it isn't it? She just doesn't want to get better. Why am I even wasting my eat me, drink me?"

"This will fix you," said her Therapist, as she reached out her hand. "Eat me, drink me."

"Eat me, drink me," said the faceless man.

"Moving on doesn't mean that you forget about her," said her Therapist. "It just means you are becoming whole again."

"Eat me, drink me," said the boy.

"Helping you be who you are again," said her Therapist.

"But, I'm an artist now," said Isobel.

"Eat me, drink me," said her mother.

"You can be whomever you want to be, all you have to do is take this," said her Therapist. "Eat me, drink me."

Isobel reached out a hand, and the world melted.

twelve : premeditated murder

The body in the king sized bed inhaled, choked, puttered, snored and continued sleeping.

She stood naked on the bed straddling the body. She could feel each individual muscle in her back work in beautiful concert as she swung the bolt cutters high over her head and down onto the head of the sleeping man.

Suspecting he might stir, she readied herself and swung the bolt cutters around and down again.

Again.

And again.

The seventh or eight time she hit his head with the cutters his head bounced off the bed and slammed into the bolt cutters with a satisfying crunch. However, this bump caused her to loose her balance and she stumbled off the bed, the bolt cutters clamoring against the floor as she landed silently in her bare feet.

She froze to the spot to see if he was going to stir.

There was silence.

He didn't stir.

He didn't breathe.

She had killed him.

thirteen : escape and taxidermy

"Excuse me," said a woman. "You're blocking the entrance to the park."

Isobel looked around to see that she had been digging in the dirt in the parking lot. Her arms were fifthly.

"Sorry," said Isobel. She wiped the tears from her face and stood up. A line of elderly men and women funneled past her.

"Don't remember you," said an elderly woman, who took Isobel's arm to keep from stumbling. "But, then again I don't remember much of anyone. You seem nice."

"I'm sorry," said Isobel. "I don't work for the nursing home."

"Fine," said the elderly woman. "But, I'm probably going to forget that as well in the next five minutes. You heading into the park?"

"I don't know," said Isobel. "I was looking for my friend Vincent, then everything unchanged for a minute, but I think I can put things back together in a new way. But, I'm not certain. I don't have the most reliable of memories."

"Well aren't we just two peas in a pod," said the elderly woman. "They tell me not having reliable memories is my mind's way of protecting me. I think it's a bunch of bullshit. I think they're using it so they can tell me whatever they want. They said that I wanted to come here. I said to them, how the hell could I even think about coming here if I'd never been here? They say, it's because of trauma. I figure if I'd been here before, and it was fun I should remember it, don't you think? I figure they're either lying about bringing us before, or it being fun. It just doesn't feel like it usually does when I can't remember stuff. Do you know what I mean?"

"No," said Isobel.

"That's alright," said the elderly woman. "I've forgotten what we were talking about anyway. I don't have the best of memories. Have you ever been here before?"

"Yes, when I was a kid," said Isobel. "I thought it was great!"

"Well, that's as good an endorsement as I think I'm going to get|," said the elderly woman. "Do you mind giving me a hand inside the gates? Or at the least through the gift shop?"

"Sure," said Isobel.

"So, what do you do when you aren't looking for your friends, or helping me?"

Isobel could still feel her raw edges. If she touched them she knew she would flinch. Like picking at a scab that wasn't ready to fall off.

"I think, I'm an artist." She wasn't used to the shape of the phrase. It tripped on back of her teeth, as she spit it out.

"Oh, I think that is something you can say with much more confidence," said the elderly woman. "There isn't enough art in the world, we need more artists, especially with that idiot in the white house. Sorry, they tell me I'm not supposed to talk about politics. I start swearing. But, don't 'think' you're an artist. Tell the world you're an artist. Scream it at anyone who'll listen. It'll be thanks to people like you that we'll make it through."

"I'm an artist," said Isobel.

"There you go," said the elderly woman. "Now, once more. Really loud!"

"I'M AN ARTIST!"

"Damn right you are," said the elderly woman.

Isobel helped the elderly woman through the open maw of the waiting concrete alligator, and into the cedar paneled gift shop and park entrance. A section of the store was devoted to souvenir spoons, thimbles, and coins. The rest was filled with stuffed alligators, young and full grown, and racist salt and pepper shakers. Isobel wondered what had happened to the dead animals in formaldehyde?

A particularly beautiful eight foot stuffed alligator was suspended from the ceiling with fishing line. Isobel craned her head around to see if the gator had a price tag.

Never know what people are looking to barter for in the frontier. Maybe I can ask on the way out.

"Ma'am," said the kid at the entry gate, "did you find your friend? Is this Vincent?"

"Do I fucking look like a Vincent?" said the elderly woman. "I can't stand it when people interject when they have no good reason too. How hard is it to say, 'enjoy your time at the park?' Fuck, I don't have that much time left and really just don't give a shit about your life story. If I did, I would take the time to ask. Do you know how much of our lives are wasted on idle chatter? Idle chatter that adds nothing to the wider discourse?"

"No," said Isobel, as they walked through the gate and onto a wooden walkway.

"Too, fucking much," said the elderly woman, loud enough for the kid to hear. "Did he hear?" she said whispering to Isobel.

"Yes," said Isobel.

"Does he look sad?"

"No, just more confused than anything else."

"Good," said the elderly woman. "Just want him to forget to ask us to pay for tickets, not scar him for life."

Isobel hadn't noticed that she didn't have to pay for her ticket.

"So you," said Isobel, "dropped all of those f-bombs so you didn't have to pay?"

"No," said the elderly woman. "I did it to see if I could. I would have happily paid, but people look at a little old lady who needs some help and everyone assumes that I'm just as sweet as their grandma. And I call bullshit! Not only was their grandma just as much of a bitch, she also dropped plenty of f-bombs in her time. You're generation didn't invent this shit! People have been fucking, cussing, drinking, and generally being assholes to one another since we walked out of our cave and realized some new motherfucker moved into the cave next door. Just because you're over seventy doesn't change that. I'm not some saint because I'm not dead yet. Self centered assholes are a pain in the ass no matter how old they are."

"Helen?" said a woman with a clipboard, as she rushed down the cedar planked walkway toward them. Isobel thought she looked more intense than she needed to be. Her hair was pulled back in a tight bun. Isobel pulled out her phone and took a quick picture.

"What are you taking a picture of?" said the elderly woman who Isobel assumed was called Helen.

"That woman with the clipboard. I have trouble recognizing what is real and what isn't."

"Oh, I can tell you, she is real," said Helen. "One hundred percent real."

"Well, that is exactly what I would tell myself," said Isobel.

"I guess you would," said Helen.

"That's the problem," said Isobel. "I'm not sure what's real and what isn't. And even if I do figure out what is real, sometimes I forget."

"Sounds exausting," said Helen. "How do you figure out what is real and what isn't?"

"The phone helps," said Isobel. "Sometimes just not caring does as well."

"Thank you for helping Helen," said the woman with the severe bun. "But, I can take her from here."

"I think my new friend wants to see the show with us," said Helen. "They bring out Goliath and a bunch of other gators and feed them. They say it's educational."

"I don't see why that would be a problem," said the woman with the bun, as she turned and continued along the walkway to a small amphitheater that was also built from cedar. Isobel and Helen followed at a much slower pace.

"They said that this is some extra charge," said Helen. "That they only do this show for special guest and tourists. I think they do it for anyone who pays enough money, and bothers to show up. I'm just going to warn you, if the seats don't have backs I'm going to have to tell someone to fuck off."

"Okay," said Isobel. She thought it was remarkable how easy it was for her to make friends now that she had decided to be an artist. It felt fantastic to be this confident and relaxed, she wondered if this was the way that most people felt when they discovered their true calling. She wondered if her mother would be proud of her. Isobel settled Helen down one of the benches.

"Fuck," said Helen. "Didn't I tell you that I would have to drop and f-bomb if they didn't have backs on these fucking benches!" Helen turned and glared at the woman in the sever bun. "She knew exactly what the fucking place was like. I could have taken a trip to the liquor store instead of sitting on this hard fucking bench."

Isobel looked around at the elderly crowd looking down on a dirt semi circle with a pair of young men in cargo shorts and tan shirts.

"Hello," said one of the men in cargo shorts, as he walked toward Isobel. "Would you be interested in helping out Ranger Tim with feeding the alligators?"

"Me?" said Isobel.

"Well, most of the other spectators don't look like they could climb down to the enclosure, and we're both scared to ask the woman who has her hair in a bun."

"I guess so," said Isobel. The only thing she was worried about was scaring off the alligators with her new found confidence. Also she knew that some wild animals could sense the monster inside her. She didn't want to spook them. But, if she was in the enclosure she might be able to keep more people safe than if she was sitting in the audience. Isobel rose and followed the young man down to the edge of the dirt semi circle, climbed over the tall cedar gate and onto a short step stool. She cautiously stepped down to the dirt and looked at the bored grey haired faces staring back at her.

"One thing," said the young man in the cargo shorts, "Ranger Tim has a tendency to get a little extra friendly with women who assist him with the feedings."

"He doesn't mean anything by it though," said the other man in the cargo shorts.

"He's really a nice guy, just really insecure about the whole-"

"Would you look what we have here," said a man who came out from behind a fence. Isobel assumed this must be Ranger Tim. Mainly because he wore a tan shirt with "Ranger Tim" embroidered on the breast pocket, just to the left of the pizza stain. Isobel thought he had a pleasant round face that belied his slight frame. "I love it when the kids pick the best of the bunch just for me."

"The what?" said Isobel.

"Oh, don't tell me they picked another one of the feminazis again!"

"I'm an artist," said Isobel.

"Fan-fucking-tastic!" said Ranger Tim. "Nothing like a chick in the arts to get the blood flowing, but I have to admit I was wondering where the smell was coming from."

"What?" said Isobel.

"Now," said Ranger Tim, changing the subject quickly, "the one thing to remember is to maintain eye contact, don't make any sudden movements or loud noises. Throw the chicken at the gator, if they decide they want to fight over it, let them. If you get involved, you become the appetizer."

Ranger Tim nodded to the men in the cargo shorts and on either side of the semi-circle a small doors opened, and alligators began advancing on them. Ranger Tim came up behind Isobel and pressed his hips against her.

"Don't run," said Ranger Tim. "Remember no sudden movements. You need to remain completely loose and calm. Breathe." He ran one hand across her hip, while brushing against her side. He walked over to one of the men in the cargo shorts who handed him a large white bucket. Isobel could see from her vantage point that it was full of chickens.

The alligators knew it was full of chickens because they began advancing toward them. Ranger Tim pulled the first chicken out of the bucket, and moved to throw it, when they heard the sound. A loud boom. Like someone had hit a car, or dropped a car from a dazzling hight. As they were searching the horizon a fighter jet flew over head. Isobel tried to see if she could figure out where it was from, but the smoke coming from the engines obscured any possibility of telling what and where this plane was from. Just before it disappeared below the tree line the pilot ejected with his parachute. Isobel looked closely at the the pilot.

"Vincent!" she called to the man in the tasteful black cocktail dress and platform shoes, as he drifted back to earth.

"Check you, Mary Lou," he called down to Isobel.

"Helen!" screamed Isobel. "That's Vincent, my best friend! Isn't he amazing!"

"The fuck is wrong with you?" said Ranger Tim, as an alligator grabbed the chicken in his hand, pulling him backwards. Ranger Tim tried to stop his fall, but instead he just dumped the bucket of raw chickens over his prone body. Before Ranger Tim had an opportunity to right himself, another alligator decided to go after one of the many chickens that had spilled out of the bucket. It chose the one that had landed on Ranger Tim's crotch.

Isobel scanned the crowd of screaming, slowly moving elderly people who for Helen.

"That's Vincent!" she screamed at Helen, once she caught her eye.

Helen sat frozen to the spot, her eyes wide with terror, as Vincent came to a graceful landing next to Isobel.

Ranger Tim continued to scream as another alligator went after another chicken.

"Did you find the woman?" said Vincent. "The one who gives the pedicures?"

"No," said Isobel.

"What the hell is wrong with you," screamed a young woman from the cedar amphitheater. "Get out of there!"

Isobel looked around and saw the alligators lumbering around in the dirt and the blood fighting over chickens. It reminded her of a story book from her childhood. There was one story about baby alligators who were trying to not be eaten by their own father. There were other details she had forgotten. But, one thing that stuck were the baby alligators distracting their father by telling hims stories.

"Do you think she might be the one who knows how to do nail art?" said Vincent.

"I'm not sure I need to know," she said. "Not, now that I'm a real artist. I mean I create art even when I'm not trying."

"Well check you," said Vincent. "Are we ready to go then?"

"In just one minute," said Isobel, as she climbed out of the enclosure and began walking toward the gift shop.

Elderly people were still screaming as they made their way back to the parking lot. Men and women who moved with an air of authority ran toward the carnage. In the chaos, Isobel strolled into the gift shop and grabbed down the eight foot alligator from the ceiling and walked out into the parking lot.

Vincent was waiting for her. She didn't stifle her joy. She held Vincent's hand as they floated into the sky.

Isobel watched a series of tiny emergency vehicles enter the dirt lot.

Vincent pointed to a patch of earth just beyond the horizon. Isobel strained to see if she could see what he was pointing to. And there, just in the distance was the Frontier. She knew it was the frontier, because it had a large sign that read, "Welcome to the Frontier!"

She turned to smile at Vincent, and realized she was sitting in a lawn chair outside a double wide trailer, her feet resting on the stolen eight foot alligator. Looking across the swirling red sand she knew she had reached the promise land.

As Isobel rose to go and tend her garden she made a not to ask Vincent if it was supposed to be, "the promise land" or "the promised land".

She looked over her garden and saw that it was all making beautiful progress. Every toe she had painted and planted has sprouted a house of worship. Tiny people of all races and creeds ran from house to house, enjoying each other's company. Except the people from the church with the white Jesus. They made their way through the crowd and apologized.

This is beautiful. I made all of this. I truly am an artist.

Isobel knew the Frontier was perfect. This was a place she could call home. It was so much quieter than the dirt lot where people were yelling at her to get down on her knees and put her hands behind her head. No one here would make her knees hurt like that. No one here would scream at here like that.

Isobel smiled and pulled her phone from her pocket. Not to take a picture of her new utopia, but to toss it away.

She wasn't going to need it anymore.

www.ingramcontent.com/pod-product-compliance
Lightning Source LLC
Chambersburg PA
CBHW022135240626
47153CB00007B/2371